David Dillon

2/1/24

The Journey of Mary Magdalene

Dave Dillon

ISBN: 1480167908
ISBN-13: 978-1480167902

THE DEATH OF MATTHIAS
(A PREFACE)

In the prequel to this book, _PROOF!_, Dr. Barry Dowell, a young theologian, took part in a secret project that sent him back to the time of Christ with the mission of finding proof of Jesus Christ and his divinity and bringing it back to Barry's time. Instead of coming back, Jesus put him to work as Matthias – the apostle elected after Pentecost to replace Judas Iscariot as a member of "the twelve". In his life as the Apostle Matthias, he wed a young girl named Shira and fathered three children. His oldest child was a son named Oded.

As Matthias, he went on missionary trips to many places, including a ten year stay in Ethiopia. His last act was as the head of the church in Smyrna, a very volatile church in a growing Roman province in what is now Eastern Turkey. The church in Smyrna went on to be one of the largest churches in the fledgling Christian emergence. Barry knew this assignment would be his last assignment and that it would take his life

This book continues the story where _PROOF!_ ends - with Barry hanging from a cross as his wife, Shira, and son, Oded, look on and he gives up his final breath. I hope you enjoy _The Journey of Mary Magdalene_ just as much as _PROOF!_.

- Dave Dillon

THE TRIP HOME

"Haven't you got a reading, yet?" barks an older, stocky, military man while staring through a pair of binoculars and lying down on the ground at the top of a ridge. A young engineer in his twenties lying next to him fiddles with an electronic scanner.

"I'm getting something… I think…" comes a nervous reply.

"You think? It's either him or it isn't!"

"It's the distance. At this range, it's difficult to pick up a strong RF reading." After a few more moments, the young man says, "I've got it. That's Dr. Dowell's signal."

"That looks like him hanging on that cross."

"I can't pinpoint where he is at this range. I can only tell you that someone down there has Dr. Dowell's RF chip under their skin."

"Well, that will have to do. I can't just go waltzing down there and ask."

After a few moments, the lad quietly asks, "What did he do to get hung on a cross?"

"What do I look like? An encyclopedia?" the military man snaps.

"Sorry! I just meant…"

"I know what you meant," he growls. "Let's get before we're spotted."

"Aren't we supposed to rescue him or something?" the young man asks alarmed.

"Negative! Our mission was to simply locate him so we can close the books on this mission once and for all. We've done that. Let's go!"

"I barely remember reading about him in the project brief when I first joined the team last year. He came here fifty eight years ago with two other guys…"

"Fifty eight years *our* time," the man replies as they start to crawl away. "We finally found the first machine about seven years ago, along with the two others on the team. They had probably been in *their* time only about one or two weeks. But Dowell had buried the two that died and then wandered off. It was decided we couldn't bring him back because he was already engaged in history and there was no way to locate him without being seen. We just needed to know he died without causing some huge ripple and we just confirmed that. Now will you shut it and keep up!"

The young lad ponders as they traverse down the backside of the ridge, "I wonder how he spent all his time here?"

"Humph, He probably spent the whole time herding sheep. Move it!" the older man barks. "We're shutting this one down like it never existed."

A group of men heave and tug at the base of the cross holding Barry's body. They finally free it enough to lay it down. Barry's body sags under its own weight. They cut him loose and several men help cover the body in a long cloth shroud and load it into the back of the old familiar wagon that brought Barry to this place. Oded then climbs up into the wagon and pulls away as Shira and a couple of the women from the church begin to wrap and prepare the body for burial.

The women attempt to comfort Shira, but the sadness in her heart is unbearable. And yet, her faith remains deep inside her. "One day," one woman begins, "God will destroy these Romans so that our men will no longer have to die needlessly."

"Needlessly?" asks Shira. "No. Matthias did not die needlessly."

"Then why?" asks another woman.

Shira stops wrapping momentarily and says, "He died for his faith. Your men... they follow Jesus, don't they? Your house? You believe in what Jesus told us?" The women nod their heads. "How much more can you believe in an idea than that you would be willing to die for it? That it's more important than your very life. That is the witness Matthias leaves you... leaves the church. Aspire to believe like him. Believe so much that your life with the Father means more to you than your life here."

"My husband and I try, but it is hard," replies the first woman.

"Yes, it is hard. But it is worth the hardship. It took me a long time to learn that," Shira answers in a hollow tone.

"It is also hard to be alone," mutters another.

"Matthias watches over me now," Shira says as she looks heavenward. "Someday I will see him again. But, yes – it hurts."

"What will you do now? Will you stay with us?" the first woman asks.

"I don't know," Shira shakes her head. "I haven't thought of that yet. There's not much I can do here now... Perhaps it is time to return to my family."

Three months finds Shira back in Timnah at the house she grew up in; the one she left to begin her life with Barry. The tears come easily and unexpectedly. She misses Barry frequently as the lonely nights still close in on her. She tosses and turns and reaches for his touch in the still of the night. The house has now officially passed to Oded and Rachel. Alon and Migda are now the doting great, grandparents to Oded's toddler and baby. Oded and Alon build a new addition onto the house so that they can all live there. Alon helps Oded when he feels well enough to swing a hammer or work the hearth, but he's slowing down and Oded does most of work. Being among family eases Shira's suffering. She goes to Jerusalem sometimes on a whim to see familiar faces, but it's just not the same.

On one such trip, Shira is staying with a friend when a knock comes at the door. The woman opens the door and after a brief conversation, invites the person in. Shira's face lights up as she sees the visitor's face.

"Andrew!" Shira exclaims.

"Hello, Shira," Andrew replies. "It is good to see you." After some pleasantries, Shira excuses the two of them and tells her friend they will return. As they walk the streets of Jerusalem, Andrew says, "I'm was so sorry to hear about Matthias."

"Thank you," Shira replies softly.

"I think about him often. I can't understand why Jesus would save me, but that Matthias should die before the rest of us. He was the smartest of the twelve. He understood Jesus better than any of us."

Shira smiles slightly, "He did get along well with the master. They spent so much time talking together."

"He should not have gone to Smyrna."

"Matthias knew what he was getting himself into. I would not have changed anything of our life together." There is a long silence so Shira decides to change the subject, "What are you doing here? The last I heard, you were going out on the road with Peter to start some new churches."

Andrew smiles, "Got sidetracked. Something came up and I actually never left. Then, when I heard you were in Jerusalem, I thought that maybe it was a sign."

"A sign of what?" Shira smirks.

"A sign that we should be together," Andrew says sheepishly.

"What?" Shira replies shocked.

"Well, you know how I have felt about you for some time now. Not that I would wish anything on Matthias for he was a brother to me. But now that he is gone, I was thinking you might consider being my wife."

"You're a sweet man, Andrew," Shira says with a big smile returning to her face. "If the circumstances were different, I would probably say yes…"

"But…" Andrew says half-heartedly.

"But, my family keeps me busy and I have been having…" Shira says searching for the words.

"Having what?"

"Dreams… feelings…. I don't know. I just feel like God has something else out there for me." She looks at the dejection on Andrew's face and adds, "I'm sorry. It's not much of a reason is it?"

"I understand," Andrew replies.

"I do care for you, Andrew. I'm just not ready for that." Shira laments.

"No. I do understand," Andrew replies. "So, tell me about Oded and Rachel."

It is a pleasant summer day in Timnah. The year that passes softens Shira's heart and she loves her life once more. She is sewing one of Oded's tunics to repair a sleeve. She hears the laughter and the voices of the young boys coming home from school. She hears the banging and pounding of Oded's hammer as he beats on a plow blade.

5

She can smell Rachel's cooking filling the house as it will soon be time to eat.

She hears the small bell outside the main door ringing. After a few moments, Rachel calls to Shira that she is needed at the door. Shira puts down her sewing and straightens her clothes. "Who could be here to see me?" she wonders as she makes her way to the door. She sees the perplexed look on Rachel's face and knows that it's someone unknown to Rachel. Shira peers around the door to see a hooded woman standing on the threshold. After a moment, the woman removes her hood and Shira's face breaks out into a large smile. "Mary!" Shira cries, "Come in, come in!" Shira grabs her arm and begins to pull her into the house.

"I'm sorry. I didn't mean to disturb you so close to dinner…"

"Nonsense. Come in here." Shira says. She turns to Rachel and says, "Rachel, this is Mary Magdalene."

"Oh," Rachel says as her perplexed look transforms into a warm smile, "I've heard a lot about you. It's nice to finally meet you."

"This is my daughter, Rachel," Shira says.

"I've heard things about you as well," Mary remarks.

Shira escorts Mary to a chair as Rachel returns to dinner. Oded comes through the door having seen someone come in. A smile breaks upon his face as well as he nods and says, "Mary, so good to see you again. You are most welcome in this house."

"Thank you, Oded" Mary replies and Oded turns to go see Rachel.

"So, what brings you here to see me?" Shira inquires.

Mary looks at her surprised and concerned at the same time. "So, you have not heard?" she asks hesitantly.

Shira's smile fades to a look of concern. "No, is there something wrong?"

Rachel appears again into the room and Mary says in a soft tone, "We can talk later."

Shria nods and then asks, "Will you stay and eat with us?"

"Oh yes," Rachel chimes in, "please stay and eat with us tonight."

"Alright, alright. I will stay," Mary says with a small smile.

The Threat

After dinner, Mary and Shira retire to the roof to sit on the old familiar bench. Shira is carrying a small folded blanket in her hands. "This old bench is where Matthias and I used to sit to watch the sunsets," Shira says softly and she sits where she had always sat. Mary comes alongside her.

"I know how much you miss him," Mary replies in a likewise soft tone.

"I know. You more than anyone understands what it is to stand helpless while the one you love is crucified," Shira says with a cracking voice. "I always bring this wrap up here with me. It was what Matthias always used in Smyrna to throw over his shoulders as he wrote. When it got really cold, he would wrap himself up in as best he could. When I hold it against my face, I swear I can still smell him. Like he's right next to me. I guess it's silly of me. But it's one of the few things of his I have left," she says as she gently strokes the top of the material.

"It's alright," Mary says as she places her hand on Shira's arm, "It will get easier in time."

"Well, you didn't come all this way to listen to me cry. What's happened? What's wrong?" Mary turns and rests her back against the bench and stares into space.

"I must leave Judah. As quickly as possible."

"Why? What has happened?"

"When my precious Jesus was with us, he told me certain secrets that he didn't tell to anyone else," Mary says in a cold, unemotional tone.

"Secrets? What secrets?"

"There were things that he said he could only entrust to my ears at the time. Some of them were hard to understand. Some of them, he told me to tell to the twelve after he was gone. Other things, I was only to tell Peter, James and John. He also told me a few things," Mary says slowly as she looks down and places her hand on the material that Shira holds, "that I will have to take to my grave."

"I don't understand," Shira responds perplexed.

"When I confronted Peter and the others with what Jesus instructed me to tell them, they became angry and accused me of inventing the whole story."

"What did you tell them?"

"It is complicated. But among other things, Jesus wanted women to be taught the scriptures and to teach and to spread the word as well as men. Peter didn't see it that way. He told me I was being silly and I needed to be more respectful and stick to my *woman* jobs."

"What did you do?" Shira asks cautiously.

"Oh," Mary says with a smile, "I got mad right back at them. What makes them think they know more about what Jesus wanted than me? I'm the one that cared for him. I'm the one he whispered to as he held me close."

"So, why do you have to leave?"

"I've been threatened..."

"Peter would never do that," Shira interrupts surprise.

"No," Mary stammers, "no. I... I don't think it's Peter or any of the remaining twelve that would make such gestures. But the fact remains that I could be in danger here. I'm leaving for Egypt."

"Egypt? That is such a long way to go." There is an awkward silence and finally Shira asks, "So, why did you come to me?"

"I want you to come with me." Mary says as she turns to look into Shira's eyes.

"Me? Why me?"

"You're one of the few people I can trust." Mary stands up and walks towards the side of the roof. The evening was closing in and there was only a sliver of moon perched low in the sky. "Matthias taught you some of the scriptures, didn't he?"

"Yes, he did. He was an… *uncommon* man in these times."

A smile crawls onto Mary's face as she coos mostly to herself, "My dear Shira, you have no idea *how* uncommon."

"What?" Shira responds, again looking perplexed.

"Never mind," Mary says with a slight chuckle in her voice. "The point is he never looked down on you."

"That's true. I don't know, I guess he treated me like…" Shira pauses looking for the words.

"Like an equal?" Mary suggests.

"Yes, most of the time. It sounds silly, but there were times when he would talk to me like he would talk to a man."

"That is how Jesus treated me, too." Mary turns to walk back towards Shira and says in a degrading tone, "Matthias was more like Jesus that Peter will ever be!"

"Mary!" Shira says shocked and raises her hand over her mouth.

"Well, it's true. And that is why I want you to come with me. Just to make sure I get there. We share a lot in common and I can trust you. You'll be back in only three or four weeks."

"It took us 4 weeks just to cross the great desert on our way to Ethiopia."

"We're not going by land, we're sailing there."

"That's expensive. I don't have that kind of money."

"I'm taking care of all of that," Mary says in a very matter-of-fact-tone. "Please come."

After a minute of rolling the idea over in her head, Shira says, "Well… I don't see why I couldn't go with you. Let me go tell Oded."

The two women enter back into the house and there is a natural curiosity from the rest of the family. "So, what is all this about?" inquires Rachel.

"Rachel!" chides Oded. "It's none of our business."

"Actually, it is," Shira says. "I'm going to go with Mary to Egypt." She holds up her hands to quiet the blurted 'but' responses to her revelation. "I'm not going to stay, I'm coming back. I'll only be gone a few weeks."

"The only way to get there and back in that time would be by sea," muses Oded.

"Yes, Mary is paying for me to go and come back."

"I want to go too. I can pay my way," demands Oded.

"What?" exclaims Rachel, "You can't be serious. You would leave me alone here?"

"No," replies Shira, "you don't have to come. I'm not going so I can explore. I'm coming right back."

"Alone?" questions Oded. "It's dangerous for a woman to make that voyage alone. Not to mention how it would look."

"I have been in more danger than a boat ride will ever be, I can take care of myself," argues Shira.

"No," interrupts Mary, "in this case I think Oded is right. There will be a lot less questions asked if there is a man with us. It would appear more proper."

"And I'm not letting you come back alone," Oded demands again.

"The boy is right," Alon chimes in as he enters the house. "If it's a long trip, you should take him. I can manage."

"She's going to Egypt…" says Rachel

"Egypt?" Alon says is a shocked tone. "Why do you want to go to Egypt? And why would you drag Oded so far away from home?"

"I'm not dragging anyone, Papa!" Shira tries to explain.

"Please!" Mary shouts. The room falls silent as everyone takes a deep breath. "Oded will come with us," Mary continues. "I'll pay his way as well. I think it would be best."

"Alright," Shira agrees.

Mary explains, "There is a ship leaving in two night's time. It carries cloth and olives to Egypt. I know the captain that sails her. We must leave tonight and travel lightly if we are to reach the port in time."

"Oded," Shira says in a more urgent tone, "ready the wagon. Rachel, help me pack, please."

"Yes, mama," Rachel says as the three of them begin to scurry about the house in preparation to leave.

After getting the wagon ready to go, Oded asks Shira, "Why is Mary leaving in such a hurry, mama?"

"It's complicated," Shira explains. "Best if we leave that for later."

"I understand," Oded says. "I'm just worried that you're putting yourself in danger."

"We'll be fine," Shira reassures him. "I'm not her protector. I'm just going with her. Just in case she needs an extra hand."

"Why does that not sound very convincing?" Oded replies skeptically.

"Have I ever given you reason not to trust me?"

"No."

"Then trust me this time and don't worry. God will watch over us."

"I'll try my best," Oded says with a big sigh.

The Flight To Egypt

It is in the mid afternoon when Alon pulls the wagon to a stop in the town of Azotus on the Palestinian coast. It is a noisy place and filled with people trading, as are most port towns. Oded helps Shira and Mary from the wagon and gathers up the few supplies they have.

"May God protect you," Alon says as he hugs Shira and kisses her goodbye. "God's speed," he says to Oded who nods.

"We'll be back as soon as we can, papa" Shira promises and that old familiar pang comes back as it did when she and Barry had to leave home.

"Thank you for everything, Alon," Mary says as she hugs Alon's neck.

Alon climbs back into the wagon and slowly pulls away as Mary, Shira and Oded make their way to the docks. "That's the ship, there," Mary says as she points to a large ship being loaded. "And that is the captain. We will need to talk to him to barter passage."

"Passage where?" Oded asks. "That ship is so full that you can barely see the deck. Where would we stay?"

"Patience, Oded," Mary says in a soft voice. "Let me do the talking."

They make their way to the loading plank and Mary asks one of the sailors to tell the captain that they wish to book passage to Egypt aboard the vessel. The sailor speaks with the captain who returns back down the plank saying, "I'm sorry, we have no room for passengers on…" He is cut off in mid-sentence as his eyes fall upon Mary standing behind Oded. He stares as his mind races and then a slight smile

14

comes to his face. "Oh, it is the Magdalene. It has been such a long time, I barely recognize you now."

"I was hoping you would not forget me," she says in a slightly flirtatious tone.

"I could never forget you, my lady. And, normally I would do anything you ask, but the cargo I carry has taken up any comfortable place I could offer you."

"I will buy out the crew," Mary says confidently.

"The whole crew? How much do you offer?"

"Two denarii… each day… for each crewman. And, of course, a bonus for you as well. But the whole crew has to sell out or it's no deal. I want privacy for myself, my sister and my nephew."

"That is quite generous, my lady. Of course, I will put it to the crew. If you will excuse me?" and the captain turns and yells for the crew to assemble as he walks back up the plank. All the men drop whatever they're doing and there is a great huddle up on the deck.

"What just happened?" asks Shira.

"It's quite common," Mary says as she turns to face Shira. "If you want a good place to sleep, you can buy a sailor's bed to sleep in and he sleeps on deck in order to make extra money. I've just offered to buy the whole crew's quarters for the trip."

"Sounds expensive," Oded quips.

"Oded!" Shira chides.

"It's alright," Mary interrupts, "he's right. But it beats sleeping standing up."

"Where will the crew sleep?" Shira asks.

"On deck. It's amazing how comfortable they can find a stack of barrels to be when they're making three times the money for the trip."

The captain returns as the crew goes back to work with a great deal of chatter. "The room is yours, my lady.

Always happy to help you any way I can. It's the door to the right," the captain says as he motions the group aboard with a smile.

"You're always agreeable if there's money to be had," coos Mary as she starts up the plank followed by Oded and then Shira.

"We sail on the next tide," the captain continues, "which will be at dusk."

Mary, Shira and Oded enter the crew quarters through a door which is so small it forces them to duck their heads. It is a bare room except for hammocks hanging at different levels between poles that run from ceiling to floor. There are slats in the outside wall to permit a little sunlight as well as some air flow into the cramped space. A thin, watery film covers the floor and there is a pungent odor of sweat and other things combined with the smell of smoke from two small oil lamps that burn with small flames. The hammocks are stained and show patches where they have been well worn. There is a hole in the floor which is the top of an angled chute which leads down to the outside of the ship. There are two dented, medium-sized, bronze buckets sitting next to the hole.

"It smells like more than a few wine and ale skins have been revisited in this place," Oded says waving his hand in front of his nose.

"Sailors are not the cleanest of people," Mary agrees, "but it's only for three days. And we will have our privacy. It's safer that way." She opens the slats to allow the maximum flow of air into the room.

The ship sails with the three gently swinging to and fro in hammocks. The sun sets and the cool night air brings a comforting relief into the small room. The stale odor from before is now somewhat replaced with a humid smell of a salty mist that kicks up from the waves just outside.

There is a lag in the conversation and Oded asks, "So if you don't mind me asking, where do you get all this money from?"

"Oh, I don't mind," Mary says as she motions to Shira who was about to speak up. "It's a fair question, Shira. Actually, Oded, my family are salt traders. My father and his two brothers own several salt mines along the salt roads to Rome. From the time I was old enough to remember, my brothers and I never wanted for money. I was the only daughter my father had and so nothing was denied me. He loved to spoil me"

"To be so lucky," Oded sighed in a distant tone.

"You're wrong," Mary corrects him. "That was my downfall. I had everything I thought I wanted... wine, exotic foods, slaves, potions and concoctions that make you forget who you are ... I was the one who became the slave. A slave to greed and pleasures of the flesh."

"I never knew that about you," Shira says.

"Few people do. I became lost in a world full of people whose job it was to wait on me. I didn't even know who I was anymore. So much of the time, it was like I was a spectator standing to the side watching myself acting the fool."

"Is that when you met Jesus?" Shira asks.

"Yes. I can't explain it. From the moment I met him, my whole life changed. I never craved for the pleasures of the world again. All I wanted to do was serve him."

"Wow," exclaims Oded, "I guess money isn't the answer to everything."

"There is nothing evil about money or possessing it. But, it can certainly lead you to a dark place if you desire it above all else," Mary replies. "The deepest desire to be

17

wealthy can be a deadly disease. And it can be fraught with demons."

"I suppose… Still," Oded reasons, "I wouldn't mind getting a *little* sick… every once and a while."

Shira laughs, "Go to sleep, Oded."

The Voyage

The first night goes quietly and the three intrepid travelers get a good night's sleep after their hard journey to get this far. Shira awakes to hear only the creaking of wooden walls as the ship pitches in the waves. She climbs out of her lightly swinging berth to find Mary missing, but Oded still soundly asleep. After taking one of the bronze buckets and seeing to the necessary, she opens the door onto deck and steps out into the brisk morning air, closing the door quietly behind her.

The crew is not very busy as they keep watch on their various responsibilities and occasionally shifting from place to place. There are a few who are sleeping on top of the cargo. The sun is still low in the sky and it cast shadows all the way across the deck. There is a slight breeze and birds can occasionally be heard above. Shira pulls her shawl tighter and walks towards the railing where Mary leans and stares out to sea. There are few places to stand because the deck is so full. Mary gives Shira a glance as she comes to the rail. "Good morning, Mary," Shira says softly.

"Did you sleep well?" Mary asks.

"Better than I expected I would, thank you. You?"

"I was more tired than I thought I would be." The two women stare out into the empty sea and there is a prolonged silence. "You know," Mary says abruptly, "I always envied you, Shira."

"Me?" Shira asked shocked. "Why would you envy me? If anything, I think I always envied you a little."

"Why me?" Mary responds with a chuckle.

"You were the closest to Jesus. You were his true love. You should have been his wife…" Shira says as her voice trails off.

"It was my pleasure to love Jesus… and my curse," Mary says as she turns around and sits lightly against the railing.

"Curse?" Shira asks perplexed.

Mary crosses her arms and begins to slowly rub her upper arms with her hands against the chill of the morning air. "As I was telling Oded, my family is in the salt business, so all my life I have never wanted for money. I guess the truth is, that growing up, I never wanted for anything. I had anything I wanted… jewelry, wine, men… As soon as I became of age, men paraded by my door."

"I'm sorry," Shira says with some shock, "I can't even imagine what that was like."

"When Jesus found me, I was lost… Consumed by the demons of greed and lust… I didn't know what true peace was until he came to me. I can't explain it to you, but Jesus was the only man that I truly loved in my whole life. And then, beyond my wildest hopes, he fell in love with me."

"Did you and he ever…" Shira says before her face blushes and she looks away.

"Oh, no," Mary responds with a grin. "No we never did. I would have with no questions, but he would not allow himself to." Then Mary adds, "Even though I believe he thought about it a couple of times." Mary starts to blush as she looks at Shira with her grin growing bigger. The two then laugh at each other's embarrassment.

"Did you ever discuss marriage?" Shira asks.

"I did… at first. But it was clear he would not allow himself that either. 'I came for the whole world,' he would say to me," Mary says as she turns around once more to stare out to sea. "'I cannot give myself to just one person.' and so I served him as his wife without ever being his wife, because I couldn't bear not to be with him."

"I never really thought about it like that," Shira says in a sad tone.

"That's why I envied you, Shira. Matthias was so much like my Jesus in the way he treated you. But you got to marry him… share his bed, give him children, hold him knowing he was yours. Now he lives on through Oded. Not being able to give myself to Jesus fully, not being able to have a child; that is my only regret from our relationship."

Shira moves to hug Mary and they embrace as Shira gains a newfound appreciation for her life and what she truly had. Just then, Oded emerges from the door with a stretch and a noisy yawn and asks, "What's for breakfast?"

Mary laughs at Oded and says, "You get to eat the bread and fruit we brought with us."

"Oh yeah," Oded says disappointed, "I forgot where we are for a moment." Now both Mary and Shira laugh. "I'm going to miss Rachel's cooking."

"You'll survive." Shira says in an insincere tone.

The captain comes towards them. As Mary looks into his approaching face, she mumbles to Shira, "That does not look like a happy man."

"I'm afraid I have some bad news," the captain begins. "It feels like a storm is coming up in the west. The ship is overloaded and I don't want to risk my payoff by venturing into any bad weather."

"We can't go back now," Oded says emphatically.

"Go back?" the captain asks is a quizzical voice. "No, that's not an option. But I'm going to save what profit I can and port early. I'll have to caravan most of the goods the rest of the way to Cairo."

"Pelousion?" Mary asks.

"Yes, that's right," the captain replies. "We'll be there by late afternoon. I'll make sure you get a spot to where you're going."

"Thank you, captain," Mary says in a disappointed tone. "We'll be ready."

Shira waits for the captain to depart and then asks, "so, where is Peleo.. Pelo…"

"Pelousion," Mary says slower. "That's the Greek name for where we're going. In Hebrew, it is simply called Sin. It means *The Strength Of Egypt*. It is on the eastern part of the Nile delta and at least an extra three days from Alexandria."

"Three more days?" Oded asks. "This is getting worse all the time."

"Oh, thank you," Mary says in a sarcastic tone which causes Shira to giggle.

"Oh, no… I didn't mean it that way…" Oded blushes. Both women begin to laugh at Oded rather than the comment.

"Come, let's get you something to eat," Shira says as she pushes him towards the door of the crew's quarters.

The ship comes to rest in the port city of Pelousion. It is a couple of hours before nightfall and the trio of intrepid travelers find food and accommodations. They are scheduled to leave with a caravan headed west in the morning, just as the captain had promised. That evening, Shira and Oded entertain Mary with stories of their last caravan adventure that took them to Ethiopia. As their excitement grows of seeing more strange animals and new destinations, Mary warns them that it may not be as great as they imagine.

The Land Of Goshen

The next morning, the three arrive at the designated spot to join the caravan. They are each assigned a camel and the final preparations are made to depart. Mary pulls out a small, clay flask and un-stoppers it. She begins to apply an aromatic lotion onto her skin. "Here," she says as she hands the flask to Shira, "you need to apply this to your skin." Shira rubs her face, neck and arms as Mary did and passes it to Oded.

Oded sniffs the flask opening and recoils, "Phew... I'm not rubbing this smelly stuff all over me."

"Suit yourself," Mary says very matter-of-factly.

The noonday sun floods the delta with light and heat. The humidity is thick and the umbrella like shade does little to add to their comfort level. Large sections of the delta are like marshland and the sounds of frogs can be heard as they try to find relief in the mud from the morning heat as well. Oded catches a glimpse of a crocodile before it scurries into some high grass.

"So what do you think so far?" Mary asks.

"It is beautiful, in its own way, I guess," Shira responds half-heartily.

"This was once farmland and pastures as far as you could see, or so the story goes anyway," Mary says. "When our ancestors were here under the pharaohs."

"Oded slaps the side of his neck and responds agitatedly, "It wouldn't be that bad except for these bugs that keep biting me!"

"They call those mosquitoes, Oded," Mary quips.

"Well, I have become their favorite meal, for some reason," he says as he slaps his arm. "Why are they picking on me?"

Shira shoots a quick look to Mary and they both begin to giggle. "What?" Oded asks.

The next afternoon brings the caravan into the land of Goshen, that ancient land of the Jewish exodus from Egypt. A noticeable ease visibly comes over Mary. As they navigate the outer city, Shira and Oded also notice familiar sounds and smells. "Wow," exclaims Oded, "I suddenly feel like I'm home."

"We *are* home, Oded," Mary smirks. "This is where Moses led us out of Egypt, but this land has always been occupied by Jews at one time or another since then." She turns to Mary and says, "I feel much better now. We have friends here."

"You must feel better," responds Shira, "you're finally smiling!"

"Am I?" Mary asks as she reaches up to touch her face.

"That may be the first one since we've left," Shira says teasingly.

"Oh, it is not."

"It's the biggest then." Shira says and then quickly turning to Oded who is eyeing some of the market stands. "Oded, keep up. We'll eat later!" Mary laughs.

The trio find themselves walking the streets looking for accommodations for the evening. Once a great caravan enters the city, the hospitality becomes cooler and places to stay become occupied quickly. As they wander down a street and are throwing out ideas, a door bursts open causing Mary and Shira to gasp and jump. A young girl comes flying out the door landing sprawled upon the ground next to Mary's feet followed closely by an angry man. "No! Papa, please..." the young girl cries.

"I will kill you!" the man says as he raises his fist.

"No!" Mary cries and bends over to put herself between the man and the girl.

"Papa!" the girl cries again.

"No!" the man cries. He looks into Mary's eyes. Mary smells the heavy veil of wine on the man's breath. He then looks around at those staring as everything in the vicinity has ground to a halt. His temper disappears and he stands erect, tries to gather his balance under the glare of the attention and says in a somewhat calmer but resolute voice, "You are no longer my daughter. You are dead to me." He turns to go back through the door and mumbles to her, "Never come back here again."

The girl sobs in a heap as Mary starts to pick her up. Shira and Oded stand motionless, not knowing what to do. Slowly, everyone returns to their previous business and there are quiet mummers. Finally Shira begins to help the girl and takes a cloth from her bag to wipe the girl's face.

"What is your name, young one?" asks Mary.

"Sarah," the girl answers through the sobs and sniffs.

"Come with us, Sarah," Mary says simply as she begins to walk away with Sarah tucked under her arm.

"Do you think this is wise?" asks Shira. "Why are you getting involved in this?"

"Would Jesus have walked away? Would Matthias?"

"No," Shira says embarrassed, "you're right. I'm sorry."

Mary shakes her head, "Let's just find a place to stay for now."

After locating a place to stay, Sarah stands in a wooden washtub while Mary helps her bathe. Sarah's body has many bruises and many of them are older than today's scuffle. "Are you hurting much?" asks Mary.

"Not such much now. Thank you for helping me. I cannot repay your kindness."

"How old are you, Sarah?"

"I just turned twelve."

"Can you talk about what happened with your father?" Mary coaxes, rubbing Sarah's back with a cloth.

"My father caught me with a boy. Micah. We love each other."

"Had you given yourself to him?"

"No," Sarah says shocked. "We had never been known to each other yet."

"I'm sorry," Mary apologizes. "Then why was you father so upset?" Sarah drops her head. Mary places a soft hand under Sarah's chin and turns her head to look into her face. "You can tell me," she insists.

"Micah is poor, like me. Papa refused to let me marry him because his family is as poor as we are."

"I see," Mary says reassuringly as she pours a small pot of warm water over Sarah's shoulders.

"Papa forbid me to see him. He wanted me to marry a tanner in town... Abram. He is so old... His wife died and he has a daughter as old as I am. He scares me more than my father. But I just had to tell Micah that it wasn't because I didn't care for him. Papa caught us together as I was trying to tell him we could never marry. He got furious and started slapping me..." her voice starting to become tense.

Mary stops her, "Shhhh. Don't speak of it any more. It's ok."

Shira enters the room carrying some clothes. "I think I found some clean clothes that will fit you," she says holding up a dress in front of Sarah. Sarah turns in the wash tub to

27

face Shira and waits for Mary to finish rinsing her off. "If these don't fit, I may have to give you some of my clothes, although I'm a little bit taller..."

"I think those will work for now," Mary interjects.

"Why are you both helping me?" Sarah quizzes.

"Listen to me," Mary says, turning Sarah around to face her. "You did nothing wrong. Being poor is not a sin. Maybe this evening, I will tell you about a man who changed the world without a denarius to his name."

It is the end of a long day that will alter Mary's life forever. They eat and then retire to sleep. Shira finally shares the 'secret of the smelly flask' with Oded as she applies ointment to the bites on the back of his neck that he cannot see.

The next day as they prepare to leave, Shira asks, "What do intend to do with Sarah?"

"We talked for some time last night. I have told her that she is coming with me to Alexandria. She is *my* daughter now."

"What?" Shira asks shocked. Mary looks confused. "I do not pretend to understand the world the way you do," Shira continues, "but if you're being sought out, would you drag this innocent girl into the situation?"

"Shira," Mary explains calmly, "you heard the father. He declared her dead to the family. By the end of today, the majority of the town will know. These are Pharisees still steeped in the old ways. No one will take her in now. I doubt even Micah's family would take her in for fear of the town's condemnation."

Shira nods her head, "Ok, I guess you know what you're doing."

Mary motions to Sarah and helps her onto a camel. "Maybe I want to help Sarah. And maybe I'm just being selfish," Mary mumbles.

"Selfish?"

"Maybe she will be the daughter that I was never able to have," Mary laments.

"Maybe both," Sarah replies. Mary nods and they both climb onto their camels. In a short time, the adventurers, now four, are off once again.

Alexandria

It is another four days of long travel until Mary's eyes rest on her ultimate destination. The great lighthouse could be seen towering above the city. "What is that tall tower?" Oded asks with the excitement of a little kid.

"That is the great lighthouse," Mary answers. "Some say it is the tallest tower in the world?"

"Is it?" Sarah asks in joyous glee.

"I do not know," Mary says with a big smile. "It's the biggest one I've ever seen. The city looks even bigger than I imagined."

"You've never been to this city?" asks Shira.

"No," Mary replies, "I've never been to Egypt. But I would listen as my father told my brothers many stories about it though."

"So if you've never been here, then what's going to happen when we arrive?" Shira asks nervously.

"Don't worry," Mary tries to assure her. "My family has many friends here. Once we get to the Jewish Quarter inside the town, we will find rest."

Another hour and they are finally walking through the Jewish Quarter. Shira and Oded are caught up in the beauty of the architecture and have not seen this large and splendid a city since they left Smyrna after Barry's death. Sarah becomes nervous among so many strange people and stays close to Mary. Mary reassures her that it will all be fine. They all stop by a large, round fountain and Mary pulls out a folded scrap of parchment and hands it to Oded. "Up this street," Mary begins to explain to Oded, "there should be a synagogue... I think it's this street... or somewhere close to this street. You should find a man there named Yostos."

"Yostos?" Oded asks sounding confused. "That sounds Egyptian."

Mary laughs, "You *are* in Egypt, remember?" Shira cannot help but giggle at Mary's comment. "Don't worry," Mary continues. "He is Jewish. Give him that note and then go with him if he asks you to."

"I will try to find him," Oded promises and starts off.

"Here," Mary says as she hands some money to Shira. "Take Sarah shopping and get her some decent clothes. Buy us some food for our meal tonight too."

"What are you going to do?" Shira asks.

Mary hugs Sarah and says to her, "Go with Shira and I'll see you back here soon." Sarah nods her head. Mary looks to Shira and says, "I'm going to look up some of my family's friends and see if I can find a place to stay. I'll meet you and Oded back here in a couple of hours."

"Alright," Shira nods her head. "Come on Sarah, let's go get some food and find you a dress... or at least some material..." She takes Sarah under her arm and heads off into the crowd.

Several dozen questions later, Mary knocks on a heavy wooden door at what appears to be a large dwelling. A small, dark-skinned woman opens the door. "Yes?"

"Is this the home of Simon Bethelanis?" Mary inquires.

"Yes. And who are you?" the woman asks.

"Would you tell him that Mary Magdalene calls."

"One moment," The woman says as she walks behind the door. Soon a taller, elderly woman pops her head around the door.

"Mary Magdalene? Is that really you?" she says as a smile crosses her face. "It's been years, dear. The last time I saw you, it was in Caesarea and you were only this tall," the woman says as she puts her hand palm-down to just above her knee. Mary smiles and nods. "Well, where are my manors? Come in. You don't need to be standing out in the busy street." Mary follows the woman into the main room as she calls, "Simon!"

"Yes, dear?" comes a voice from another room.

"Come see who is in your house," the woman beckons.

An elderly man comes into the room and stops. After staring at Mary and trying to place her, he says, "Is that a Magdalene? Mary was it?"

"You remember me?"

"Not so much," he says as he crosses the room to hug her. "But you look so much like your mother when she was younger. And I can see a lot of your father in you too. The last I saw your father was probably in Caesarea when we closed that big salt contract. I guess you were with him. How is your father?"

"He died six years ago," Mary says sadly.

"Oh, I'm sorry to hear that. How is your mother?"

"She is doing well. She's living with my oldest brother."

"Good. So, what can an old man do for the daughter of a really good friend?"

"I've come here to try and make a new start, and I need a place to stay."

"A new start? Did something terrible happen?"

"My… fiancé died suddenly…"

"Oh, that is terrible," the woman says.

"And my dad always talked about this city and it sounded like a place where I really wanted to live, so…"

"Oh, you will love this city, dear," the woman blurts out. "It has everything that anybody could possibly imagine." She turns to the elderly man and says, "Simon, she could stay in that little house down by the big fig tree."

"Well, I suppose…" the man utters.

"Nobody lives there," the woman interrupts, "because it's just too small for a family. You don't have any children, do you?"

"I just have one daughter – she's adopted," Mary adds.

"Well then, you can sleep in the same room. It'll be perfect. Come dear, I'll show you which one it is. I'll be right back, Simon."

"Good bye, Mary," the man is able to get out before the woman drags Mary out the door.

"It's getting close to sunset," Oded says to Shira as they sit by the fountain. The bustling crowd from earlier in the day is starting to thin out.

"I know, son. She'll find us. She said to meet here."

"Is this where all of us are going to live?" asks Sarah.

"Where you and Mary will live," explains Shira. "Oded and I have a home near Jerusalem."

"Jerusalem!" Sarah exclaims wide-eyed. "You live in Jerusalem?"

"Not in Jerusalem, but close. My home is called Timnah. It's about two days travel from Jerusalem."

"Have you been to Jerusalem?" Sarah asks.

"Yes. I've been many times. I have lots of friends there."

"I've always wanted to see Jerusalem."

"Maybe someday you will," Shira says as she strokes Sarah's hair.

"Have you been to the temple?"

"Yes. I was there with Jesus and Matthias. Matthias was my husband and Oded's papa."

"Wow," Sarah sighs with a big smile on her face.

"I'm here," Mary announces as she walks up on the group.

"It's about time," Oded announces, "I'm getting hungry!"

"Oded!" Shira admonishes and Mary laughs.

"Come," Mary says as the others get up to follow, "I've found the perfect little house for Sarah and myself. It will be crowded with the four of us, but we'll make due. Come, this way." Mary points off to the distance with one hand and reaches out to Sarah with the other.

They enter the dwelling and a single oil lamp bathes the room in a weak, but soft light. It is a single barren room with a kitchen area at one end. There are a couple of chairs but no table. There is an uncovered doorway to the side from the entrance that leads to a small room with a double bed with no linens or pillows. A small chest rests in the corner alongside Mary's things. There is only one pot for cooking, so they borrow another one from the neighbor. It's not a large place, but it's not as cramped as Mary said it would be. But everyone is determined to make the best of it.

After eating, Mary and Shira sit in the chairs almost facing each other. Oded lays on the floor and Sarah sits on the floor between Shira and Mary. "Oh," Mary blurts out as a thought comes to her, "did you find Yostos, Oded?"

"Yes," Oded groans like a person who has just eaten too much. "I showed him the note and he said 'I'll take care of this'. That's all he said and I left."

"That's fine," Mary replies. "Thank you for doing that for me."

"Not a problem," Oded answered; curious as to what it was all about. But he knew it wasn't really any of his business and knew better than to ask.

Sarah finally asks, "Mary, is this where I will live from now on?"

"Well," Mary says slowly and drawing a big breath, "I would like to take you in as my daughter. I promise to treat you kindly and I'll teach you anything you don't already know. Would you like to live here with me?"

A smile floods onto Sarah's face. "I would like that a lot," Sarah beams.

"Your twelve now," Mary continues. "In another year, you will be of age. We will see what you already know and I will teach you how to keep a proper house. There will be lots of eligible boys here in Alexandria."

"I can cook some things," Sarah explains excitedly. "And I can sew my own clothes and mend too."

"That is a good start," Mary says with a smile.

"So, you don't have any children?" Sarah asks.

Once again, Mary draws a deep breath. She looks at Shira and, for a very brief moment, a remorseful look crosses Mary's face. But it disappears quickly and Mary holds out her hand inviting Sarah to come sit a bit closer. Then in soft voice, she says, "Let me tell a story about a man named Jesus…"

Short Lived Dream

Shira and Oded stay for another three days helping Mary get settled in. But Shira was missing Timnah and Oded was tired of sleeping on the floor. As much as they enjoyed being with Mary and Sarah, it was time to go home. It was a sad goodbye, as they stood next to the boarding plank.

"Thank you for everything, Shira," Mary says as she hugs Shira tightly.

"It was my pleasure," Shira responds.

"And thank you, Oded. You've been a big help," Mary says as she hugs Oded.

"Thank you for the adventure," Oded smiles.

"Take care of her, Sarah," Shira says as she hugs Sarah's neck.

"I will," Sarah smiles.

"You'll be safe here," Shira says to Mary. Mary nods.

"The tide is made," the captain calls from the galley. "Come aboard, please."

"Come on, Oded," Shira says. "It's time to go."

"God go with you," Mary calls after them.

"You too," Shira responds. "I'll miss you."

They all wave as the ship begins to pull away from the dock. Mary and Sarah stand and watch the ship until it is several hundred yards off shore.

"Let's go home," Mary says in a very contented voice as she puts her arm around Sarah and they stroll away from the dock.

36

The next few months goes by quickly for Mary. She has her hands full with Sarah and her education. Sarah is good at many of the skills that women were *responsible* for doing. But she has little knowledge of men in general or how to be a good wife and mother, and not just a cook and seamstress.

"So your mother never told you much about boys?" Mary asks nonchalantly.

"My mother died when I was eight," Sarah replies.

"Oh, I guess we never talked about her, did we? So who taught you how to cook and sew after that?"

"Ruth, the woman who lived next to us."

"Oh. So it was just you and your father?"

"And my brother. But he got married and moved out when I was ten."

"So you took care of them after your mother died," Mary says mostly to herself.

"Yes. That is also when papa started drinking all the time. Ruth told me it was because he missed mama. My brother told him he needed to stop. He told the rabbi about it too. Then the rabbi came and talked to my father."

"But it didn't help, did it?" Mary interjects.

"No. He told my father that my mother must have committed a great sin to die so young. He said my father was probably responsible." Sarah explains in a hollow voice. "It made him drink more. Then he started to beat on my brother. That's why he left when he got married. After that, he started hitting me."

"I'm sorry," Mary laments.

"That's why he wanted me to marry Abram instead of Micah. He said it would save me from dying like my mother." Sarah explains.

"Listen to me," Mary says, "it doesn't work that way. Your mother didn't die because she committed a terrible sin. Your father was just confused. Do you understand?" Sarah nods. "Remember what I told you about Jesus? You don't have to be afraid of God. He loves you... and I love you." Sarah smiles and hugs Mary with all her strength. "Now," Mary continues in a soft voice, "let's talk about boys..."

Mary also takes it upon herself to teach Sarah the scriptures as Jesus had taught her. The two of them bond quickly and soon, Sarah begins to refer affectionately to Mary as 'mother'. It makes Mary's heart float every time she hears it.

Yostos is a disciple of Jesus living in Alexandria and helps Mary connect with other disciples in the area. There is great excitement within the community that Mary is among them. Because of her small home, she and Sarah would go to other's homes to break bread, tell stories and remember the teachings of Jesus. They constantly seek Mary out to ask questions and acquire advice. She begins a small church that meets in homes around the area and their lives start to become normal.

It has only been a short eight months since Mary and Sarah have taken up residence in Alexandria, and the time is packed with new discoveries and experiences. They explore their new city and make new friends. Sarah is drawing the attention of several boys in the town as she becomes quite the young woman. She also is becoming very familiar with the teachings of Jesus. Mary learns that she is a very bright and curious young woman and learns very quickly.

It is a warm spring day. The humidity is high, but there is a cool breeze coming off the sea that holds the sun's heat in check and makes the day comfortable. Mary is cleaning and Sarah sits at the loom as the sound of a bustling city invades through the windows and the smell from the nearby fig trees wafts in the air. There is suddenly an urgent knock at the door. Mary dries her hands on her apron and moves to answer the summons as Sarah looks up from her work. When Mary opens the door, she is stunned and can't believe her eyes. The man and woman who stand before her threshold shock her back into her earlier life. A life full of love and turmoil. A life with Jesus.

"Lazarus? Martha?" Mary asks in a shocked tone of unbelief.

"Hello, Mary," Lazarus says.

The joy of seeing old friends is mixed with an anxiousness that something is amiss for them to be here. After an awkward silence, Mary says, "Well... come in." Then tuning to Sarah, she says, "Sarah, bring some fruit and wine for our guests." Sarah moves the loom out of the way and then hurries over to the kitchen portion of the room as Lazarus and Martha enter the small home. The three sit and Mary says, "I can't believe you're here."

"We arrived in Alexandria yesterday," Lazarus explains, "but it took us a while to find you."

"I told Lazarus we need only to find the church here and we would find you," Martha adds.

"But you did find me, that's what's important," Mary chirps. "Is Mary with you?"

"No," Martha replies. "She remained in Bethany to look after things."

Sarah returns to the table carrying a platter of fruit slices and places in the center. She heads back to the kitchen area.

"And who is this?" Lazarus asks after Sarah.

"This is Sarah... my daughter," Mary beams. The pronouncement leaves both Lazarus and Martha with confused looks.

"*Daughter*?" Martha asks quietly.

Sarah brings the wine carafe and some clay glasses to the table. Sarah takes the last chair, scoots it near to Mary and then sits. Mary reaches to stroke Sarah's hair. "Her family cast her out. I have taken her in as my daughter."

The looks of confusion disappear and Lazarus says, "Ah, well, we are very happy to meet you, Sarah." Sarah nods shyly. He pours himself and Martha some wine and takes a wedge of fruit.

"How was your trip?" Mary asks as she attempts to make conversation.

"Interesting," responds Lazarus. "It's the first time either Martha or I have been on the open sea."

"I thought I was going to be sick at first," Martha adds. "But after a day, I was better."

"I'm so happy to see you," Mary says, "but I'm afraid to ask you why you're here."

"It's Peter," Lazarus states.

"Is he sick?" Mary asks after rolling her eyes. "Or, is it something he's done?"

"It's something he's going to do," Martha blurts out.

After looking at Martha, Lazarus says hesitantly, "He going to Rome."

"*What*?" Mary exclaims as she bolts to a standing position.

"I know," Lazarus empathizes, "just remain calm."

"Calm?" Mary asks as she starts to pace the floor talking out loud to nobody in particular. "Jesus shared with me the things he couldn't tell the twelve at the time. Telling me to tell Peter after he was gone. And I told Peter... one thing that Jesus was really clear on was that none of us were to go to Rome. He said that someone from the next generation would go to Rome, once a great evil there had passed."

"A great evil?" Martha asks.

40

"He did not say what it was, but he did say it would bring down the Romans on our heads... more than they already are." Mary continues to pace. "The persecution would be terrible and no one would be safe. That man can be so mule-headed sometimes..."

"What did Peter say when you told him?" Martha asks.

"Oh, he didn't believe me. He never believed me. When I told him Jesus wanted me to be a disciple and help him teach, he kept saying that women shouldn't be disciples. Peter said I was over reacting and how I was just a *noisy woman*," Mary says as she throws her hands up in the air. "That's why I asked you to watch him, Lazarus. I knew he was going to do this."

"Well," laments Lazarus, "there's nothing we can do about it now."

"I can go and stop him before he gets there!" Mary says as she stops pacing.

"What?" Martha exclaims

"It's too late. He left about the same time we did," explains Lazarus.

"Was he going by land or sea?" Mary asks.

"Land. Of course he was going to stop at a couple of churches along the way."

"Then I can sail to Rome and be there to meet him." Mary turns to Martha, "Can you watch over Sarah while I'm gone?"

"No!" Sarah exclaims as she jumps up. She embraces Mary tightly with her head lying upon Mary's chest and says, "Don't leave me. I want to go where you go."

"It will be dangerous, child."

"I don't care. I want to come with you."

"No. If Jesus said not to go, then why would you also go to Rome?" Lazarus interrupts.

41

"I have a chance to stop Peter from making a terrible mistake." Mary pleads.

"Now who is being mule-headed?" asks Lazarus.

"It's important, Lazarus. I have to go."

"I'm coming too," Sarah says

"As am I," Lazarus adds.

"As my protector? I can take care of myself," Mary says.

"As a good friend," Lazarus replies.

"You don't have to come with me."

"Since everyone else is being mule-headed, it is my turn," Lazarus says defiantly.

There is a pregnant silence as they look at each other. Grins begin on their faces, which turn into smiles, which in turn leads to laughter.

"Ok," Mary agrees, "then we will all go together." She raises Sarah's head in her hand and strokes Sarah's face and hair. "Who knows," Mary laments, "it may take all of us to get through this. But if we are going, we must hurry."

As it turns out, *hurry* is not in the cards. It is another three days before there is a galley sailing from Alexandria to Rome. The four board the ship and settle in for a journey that will take a week; as long as the winds hold and with several stops along the African coast.

The Crossing

The galley bids farewell to the African coast and slices into the deep blue-black water headed to the other side of the Mediterranean and the coast near Rome. There are eight others that sail with them, two of which board at the last port. It is a three day journey and two days pass without incident. The third day is a gray, overcast day with a cool, stiff breeze from the west as the waves buck the large galley up and down. The large sail strains against the yardarm and the mast creaks ever so slightly. The pennants snap loudly in their chaotic dance. Once again Mary finds herself standing next to a railing and staring out into the open bleakness.

Lazarus walks up behind Mary and reaches an arm around her shoulders, "Warm enough? Shall I get you a shawl?"

"No, I'm fine," Mary says snapping out of her trance with a smile.

"The wind seems a little stronger than the past few days. Is this normal?"

"I don't know. I've never been in these waters before. The sky doesn't look too bad. What were you doing?"

"*Bah,*" Lazarus scoffs, "Martha and Sarah were talking endless woman stuff. I needed a break."

Mary laughs. "You poor man," she says sarcastically.

"How long until we get to Rome?"

"I'm guessing we'll dock sometime tomorrow. Then the rest of the day to get into Rome. We'll need to keep a low profile and search for Peter at the same time."

"I wonder if Rome will be any more hostile for us than Jerusalem was."

"Less hostile, from what I've been told."

"*Less?*" Lazarus asks in a shocked tone.

"Yes. In Jerusalem, we have to deal with the Pharisees who see us a large threat to their power and hold on the people. From what I understand, the Romans have bigger problems. They consider us just an annoying flea. Which is why going to see the emperor is a bad idea. If Peter says the wrong thing, we could draw more persecution to ourselves, not less."

"It's bad enough already," Lazarus laments.

Mary looks into Lazarus' eyes, "It will get worse before it gets better. Jesus told me that." After studying the look of concern on Lazarus' brow, she gently reaches up to stroke his face and says with a smile, "You're right. It is getting colder." With the tension of the conversation momentarily broken, both of them laugh softly.

"Do you need a shawl?"

Mary shakes her head and says with a smile, "We'll go below and I'll see if I can get Martha and Sarah to talk about something else."

Lazarus laughs. But it quickly fades as he looks away, "The sky is darkening. I don't like it."

"We'll be fine," Mary assures him, "Let's go below." As they head for cover, Mary says, "I just hope nobody gets sick with all this bouncing."

Lower clouds roll in a few hours later. The sky darkens even more and the wind picks up. The ship is heaving to and fro. Food cannot be served so everyone is given bread and wine, but few eat it. There is a morbid foreboding that grips everyone onboard. Everyone is holding onto something to keep from being tossed around. Then the rain comes. It falls in sheets and is driven with such force that it can be heard below the deck. Thick trickles of water are forced under the doorway and water drip on their heads through small cracks in the deck. Thunder and lightning join in the chaotic chorus and Mary begins to pray for deliverance. Suddenly, the door flies open and the captain clings to the jamb and yells, "Everyone on deck! We're taking too much water!" It is hard to hear him as the wind howls and the rain seems to move almost horizontally in the flashes of light that silhouette the captain's torso. There is confusion and then a hesitation as the captain continues to shout and tries to pull the closest people out the door. As people stumble onto the deck, they're given wooden buckets and deep wooden bowls and bronze pots. The water comes pouring in the opening as Mary climbs the small steps to the door. It is not quite night and there is a hint of light that still remains. The water is ebbing from one side of the deck to the other as the ship rolls and rocks from ankle deep to almost knee deep in waves. People are being knocked down over and over by the water as they struggle just to stand. The sail had been gathered up but large sections have torn and are now whipping tattered and shredded as the wind tries hard to rip it away from the ropes holding it.

"Bail!" is the cry that keeps echoing in a faint rhythm through the deafening wind and rain. The crew are better at bailing and most of the passengers make no difference in the amount of water coming on deck. It is a losing battle and everyone can see it. The sail then breaks the ropes holding it and a large section jumps into the wind and it is held by only a small section to the mast. The force tips an already unstable ship to the point where one of the sides begins to be submerged under the water. People are now leaning or stooping just trying to hold their footing; some try to push to the higher railing. A great wave comes washing over the deck sweeping away half the people standing along with it. In the receding of the water, five people are dragged into the sea. The ship continues to list in the direction of the tugging sail. There is a great confusion and people begin to scream out and flail in the churning water. Mary grabs hold of Sarah just as the next wave leaps onto the deck taking all four of them and a couple of the crew into the sea. Out of the corner of her eye, Mary sees the longboat tied to the stern of the galley.

"The boat…" is all Mary can get out before a wave consumes her and Sarah. Once their heads are again momentarily above the water, Mary yells, "Swim!" and yanks on Sarah. Lazarus finds Martha and yanks her in the direction of Mary. The boat is not far, but it seems unreachable. As they swim, the boat seems to dance closer and then farther away with each wave that crashes over their heads. Almost beyond belief, Mary and Lazarus reach out and grab the edge of the boat. Another wave crashes against them but the boat holds them above the crest. They pull Sarah and Martha close enough that they can get a handhold on the side as well. They manage to pull, push and lift each other into the boat. It is exhausting and Mary feels as if her muscles are burning, but it's not over yet. She yells, "Bail!" and picks up a small pail tied to the boat. She begins emptying the water out of the small boat as quickly as she can. Lazarus spots others trying to get to the boat. Mary hands the pail to Sarah and tells her to bail. Martha also finds a pail and begins to bail. Mary reaches for the two others trying to climb into the boat. As one woman begins to clear the side, there is a loud crack. The small sail breaks away and snaps the mast off with it. It glances off Lazarus' head nearly knocking him back in to the water. It catches the woman squarely on her upper body and knocks her into the water; dragging her away from the boat and beneath the waves. Sarah screams and begins to panic, trying to stand up. Mary grabs her and wrestles her down.

When she can see Sarah's eyes, she yells, "It's ok… it's ok… keep bailing." Sarah begins to calm down and nods her head and goes back to bailing. Mary and Lazarus help the man who is still holding the side into the boat. Lazarus has a gash in his head and is bleeding. Once the man is in, Mary takes her dress and tries to stop the bleeding.

"I'm ok," Lazarus yells.

"You're bleeding. Hold still," Mary replies

The man drags himself to the back of the boat and grabs the rudder handle. It moves freely back and forth. "The storm has snapped off the rudder," he yells. "We're going to die!"

"Only if it is God's will," Mary yells. "Keep bailing!"

Mary takes the pail from Sarah as her arms begin to tire. The man takes the pail from Martha. Mary then notices that the small boat is still tied to the galley. "Lazarus," Mary yells pointing to the front of the boat, "The rope!" Lazarus drops the bucket crawls to the front and takes out a small knife and begins sawing at the rope. "Hurry, Lazarus!" Mary screams as the galley begins to go under. The rope suddenly snaps and the boat pitches up, tossing Lazarus onto his back into the center of the boat. Sarah reaches for Lazarus and tries to stop his gash from bleeding.

It is a long night as they bob up and down on the waves, bailing and taking on the occasional wave that tries to slap them from the boat. After the minutes stretch into hours, the rain dies down. The waves become manageable. The weather seems to depart as quickly as it appeared and an exhausted Sarah falls asleep in Mary's arms as the rest of them sit dazed and stare into the darkness.

"What is that sound?" Mary thinks. "It sounds like a bird... It is a bird... a very loud bird!" She opens her eyes as the fog recedes from her mind and the sunlight becomes painfully bright. She shields her eyes and they begin to focus. There is a seabird squawking on the front of the boat. "It *is* a loud bird," Mary says out loud. As she starts to sit up, the bird takes wing and flies away into the sky. Her movement disturbs Sarah, who also begins to wake up. Mary is stiff and her back hurts from where she was leaning against one of the seats in the boat. She rises up from the bottom of the boat wet and cold because there is still a large amount of water still in the boat. She begins to look around. They are adrift and only a watery horizon can be seen in every direction.

"Where are we?" asks Sarah as she surveys the situation.

"There's no way to tell," Mary replies.

Mary shakes Martha, "Martha?"

Martha slowly wakes up and is also stiff and sore. She stretches as she utters, "We're still alive."

Lazarus and the man are also starting to stir. As Lazarus opens his eyes and begins to move, Mary tries to restrain him, "You're injured, you should lie still."

"Am I pouring blood?" Lazarus asks in a skeptical voice?

"No," Mary replies confused.

"Then, get off me woman and let me up," Lazarus says in a cantankerous manner.

Mary smiles and helps Lazarus to a sitting position. "There's no way to tell where we are," Mary reports.

"Well, we're alive. That's always a good start to the day," Lazarus says as he stretches.

"But for how long?" the unknown man asks dejectedly. "My name is John by the way. Thank you for saving me."

"That poor woman," Sarah mumbles.

"That was my wife," John mumbles.

"I'm sorry," Mary says.

There is a long silence as the boat gently bobs in the water under a sun that sits high in the sky.

"What do we do now?" asks Sarah.

"We have no food and nothing to fish with," Lazarus says. "Our mast is gone and our rudder has snapped off, so we can only drift with the current. We are in God's hands now."

"Then we should pray," Mary replies. She kneels in the boat and raises her hands to the sky, "My sweet Jesus. I should have listened to you. Forgive me. And do not hold these others responsible for my sins. If it is the father's will that we live, then deliver us to safety. If it is the father's will to call us home, then come to us quickly, sweet Jesus, that we should not suffer. For I know you watch over us without ceasing."

"Who is this Jesus that you pray to?" John asks.

With no other pressing matters, Mary, Lazarus and Martha take turns telling their own stories of Jesus to John. Sarah is particularly fascinated with Martha's tales. It helps pass the time and they forget for a while how hungry they are. They take turns bailing as much water as they can and both the boat and their clothes completely dry out before dusk. As day falls and the sun slowly sinks into the sea, they are still of good spirits. They are able to adjust their positions where they can be as comfortable as possible. It is a chilly night, but because they were able to dry out, they are not as cold as they were the night before. But it is still difficult to sleep. The small boat bobs now in the pitch blackness. There is no moon tonight. The sky is a star-encrusted canopy, but offers little light to see by. There is a deathly silence only disturbed by the sounds of the tiny splashes of water against the side of the boat and the occasional cough, snort and snore from the occupants.

The sun rises on another day and still there is no land in sight. This day passes much more slowly as the conversation drags and weakness begins to overcome them. The hope for a rescue starts to fade as there are no other ships that pass within sight. As the night closes in around them once more and they prepare to sleep to escape the hunger and thirst for a few hours, Sarah whispers, "I was dreaming of Matthew last night."

"Matthew... Matthew?" Mary whispers back. "Is he the stonecutter's son?"

"No. Matthew is the son of Amos, the carpenter. Down by the square."

"Oh, yes. The tall one."

Sarah nods. "He always looks at me when I go for water. I think he likes me."

"And you like him?"

"Maybe," Sarah says with a soft giggle.

"*Maybe*? You ignore two other wells that are closer so you can go get water outside his father's shop and you say '*Maybe*?'" They both giggle.

"He's so cute. And I have talked to him a couple of times."

"He is cute. What did you talk to him about?"

"Oh... just stuff."

"I see..."

50

"I think I would like to be married to him," Sarah whispers hesitantly.

"You would make him an excellent wife."

"Will I ever see him again?"

"You may. Because of our relationship with Jesus, there is always hope. Never forget that."

"Maybe I will dream of him tonight too," Sarah sighs.

"You do that. Sleep well," Mary whispers with a smile.

A New Land

"Mama, wake up," Mary hears Sarah say as she's jolted awake. Mary opens her eyes and can only see a panicked Sarah. "Look!" Sarah shouts. Mary quickly sits up and turns as the others are waking from Sarah's alarm. The very nose of the boat sets beached on a rocky coastline as the waves roll onto shore holding the small boat in place. As she looks around, the others now see the same sight also.

"We made it!" exclaims Lazarus. "Lord, be praised!"

"I thank you, Lord!" squeals Martha.

Mary climbs out of the boat and wades through the ankle deep water to the shore. Sarah comes alongside her and she puts her arm around Sarah.

"I told you," Mary whispers, "there is always hope."

Mary calls the others into prayer for their deliverance and then they begin to look around for clues as to where they are. The shore is barren and there is no sign of civilization.

"This vegetation doesn't look familiar at all to me," Mary says.

"We could be anywhere," Lazarus adds. "The sea is to the south, so we must have made it across. The only question is - which way to the people?" Lazarus looks to Mary and notices she is standing quite still. He walks to her and says, "What is it?"

"Look!" she exclaims as she points to a small cleft in the inclined rock face. Everyone stops and looks and, there in the distance, a small boy stands on one of the lower precipices staring back at the group. "Hello!" Mary yells as she waves her arm in a big arcing motion. The boy lingers a few seconds and then disappears.

"Well," John says, "I hope that is not an omen of the welcoming committee."

The group chuckles as Lazarus points after the boy, "I guess we go where he goes."

"And hope they're friendly," John adds.

The group makes their way up the rock incline towards where they saw the boy. It is a slow climb. "Did you recognize what the boy was wearing, Lazarus?" asks Mary as her feet pick their way through the stones on the ground as they climb the hill.

"It looked like animal hide to me," Lazarus responds.

"Me too. We must be in some primitive area. We can't be too close to Rome," Mary continues.

"It could be just a small outlying village or town. There's no way to know."

"I hope they have food," Sarah says.

"I've never been to the end of the earth, but I think this is it," Martha says as she struggles to keep up.

They find a way to the top through the small cleft and it opens into a large valley. The landscape is like nothing they've ever seen.

"This is beautiful," exclaims Martha.

"I have to agree," says Mary.

"Look," shouts Sarah, "Fig trees!" She runs to the first tree and picks some low hanging figs. Everyone else makes their way to a tree and begins to munch on the fruit.

"Oh, this is so good," Mary says.

"They're sweeter than any figs I've ever eaten," Martha says.

"I think they could be rotten and they'd still taste good to me," Lazarus exclaims.

The group laughs. After a couple of handfuls of figs, everyone is feeling much better. Lazarus notices a group of people coming, mostly men. "Mary," he announces as he points to them, "here comes the welcoming party."

The group assembles just outside the trees and waits for those walking towards them. There are a dozen men, who are dressed similar to the boy they saw, followed by a woman. They are lightly armed with spears, but seem to be more curious in their posture and tone than threatening. The boy hops sideways excitedly as he leads them while looking back and forth and talking and pointing. Mary cannot make out what the boy is saying.

"They don't look aggressive," John notes. "Let's hope they don't own the fig trees."

After they approach, the two groups stand in a moment of silent observation. "Hello?" Mary offers. One of the men says something, but it is incomprehensible to the group. "Oh dear," Mary utters, "it seems they don't speak Greek." Mary tries to say hello in Aramaic and Hebrew with no success. As the men talk among themselves, the five outsiders can only stare as none of it is recognizable. The leader of the group makes a '*come with me*' motion and starts to walk away. He stops when no one in Mary's party moves and makes the motion more forcefully.

"Should we follow him?" Mary asks.

"We have few options. Come on," Lazarus says and begins to follow. Mary grabs Sarah and begins to follow Lazarus. The five of them are enveloped by the group of men as they are lead off to an unknown destination.

They come to a small village which becomes all abuzz upon their arrival. Everyone is talking and pointing as they stare at the strangers. The man who led them to the village walks to a tent, pulls back the flap and motions them inside. Lazarus enters, followed by the others and the flap is closed. It is a square tent with a rough-hewn, wooden table in the middle large enough for all of them to sit at. It is surrounded by simple wooden benches with no backs. In the center of the table is a wooden pole which sits in a small cavity in the table top and goes to the top of the tent to support the center. There are blankets of both cloth and hide piled in several heaps. As they look around, Lazarus says, "Ok, so now what?"

"Well, I'm going to sit down," John says very matter-of-factly. "I'm still hungry. I wonder if they will feed us."

He doesn't have long to wonder. As they start to sit at the table, the flap opens again and several women pour into the tent carrying bowls and plates of food. As they set the plates and bowls on the table, Mary once again calls them into prayer to bless the food. She speaks in a whisper, but she raises her voice several times to be heard over all the concurrent conversations of the others in the tent observing them. There are meats, vegetables and stews which look, smell and taste totally foreign to them. But at this moment, they don't question. They happily eat, and there is enough food that they are all able to eat until they are full.

When one of the women reaches in and holds up a bowl in a manner of urging them to take more, several of the group groan and wave their hands to signal that no more is required. At that point, the women begin to remove what is left of the food and the table is cleared. After the cacophony of the meal, the tent suddenly falls silent and the group is left to contemplate what has transpired.

"I am so full," Lazarus says.

"I loved that reddish stuff," Sarah melts. "What was it?"

"I have no idea," Mary replies. "But I loved it too. I've never had anything like that."

"Those were beets," John replies. "I've only had them a couple of times in Alexandria, although they were never prepared like these were. They're rare and hard to find back home." After looking around the tent in a futile effort to see something different, John adds, "So, what now? What are we going to do now?"

"I vote for a nap," Lazarus says with a smile. Mary nods her head.

"No. I mean, where do we go from here?" John demands. "How are we going to get to Rome? We can't talk to these people."

"Calm down, John," Mary says with upheld hand. "We will find our way in time."

"But I don't have time," John says growing more impatient. He goes over to the flap and opens it. Not seeing anyone nearby, he walks out and the flap falls closed again.

"Impatient, isn't he?" asks Lazarus.

"He just lost his wife and he's scared," Mary explains. "I'm not sure that I blame him. We are also running out of time, Lazarus."

"You think we can still catch Peter?" Martha asks

"I don't know," Mary responds. "But, we are here and there is no telling when we will find our way, so we just have to keep positive."

John flings the flap open and steps back into the tent, "It's impossible. These people don't understand anything. They can't give us directions."

"The sea is to the south, so we know that we're somewhere on the northern coastline," Lazarus explains. "Rome is either to the east or to the west. We have an even chance of guessing it right." Martha rolls her eyes and Lazarus' comment seems to placate no one, least of all John.

Evening comes and the women reenter the tent to move the benches and lay out the blankets on the ground for sleeping. There are some crude pillows buried underneath the piles of blankets. The village settles in for the evening and the group now sits on the ground. The tent is lit by a single pot which contains some sort of grease or fat which fuels a medium-sized flame.

"I'm leaving tomorrow morning. I have to get out of here," John announces.

"I don't think that's a good idea," Martha contemplates. "I've been thinking. What if there are wild animals out there. You saw the spears and what they wear. We might need weapons."

"I don't care," John says. "We have to get out of here."

"Martha is right," Lazarus says. "We need to find a way to convince some of the men to accompany us... for protection."

"How?" John asks. "They don't understand anything we say."

"Tomorrow, after breakfast," Mary says, "we will try again. We will have to figure out a way to tell them where we want to go."

"Why don't we draw them a picture? A map?" Sarah asks.

"They're too primitive," John exclaims. "They probably don't know what is more than a league from here."

"Actually, that's a very good idea, Sarah," Mary says. "It's the best idea we've had yet. We'll try it tomorrow. Let's get some sleep." Everyone settles under their blankets and Mary blows out the flame.

The next morning, Mary and Lazarus are stirred by noises outside the tent. As they begin to move around, Mary wakes Sarah and Lazarus wakes Martha.

"Where is John?" Lazarus asks.

"He's probably outside trying to make them understand he's about to unravel," Mary says with a chuckle.

Mary, Martha and Sarah begin to fold the blankets and stack them in a much neater pile than they were the day before. Lazarus moves the benches back to the table and it is not long before they are served breakfast. Once breakfast is over, Mary leads the delegation of four out of the tent, and into the main area of the village next to a large bonfire. The man who escorted them approaches as Mary pick up a stick from the dirt.

"Ok," Mary says as she takes a slow breath and smiles back to Sarah, "let's give this a try." She gets the man's attention and begins drawing in the dirt with the stick. "This is the Roman territory as I remember seeing it on a map," Mary says to no one in particular as she draws. "This is the sea," she says as she scratches wiggly lines in the dirt, "and Rome is somewhere around here..." She then looks at the man. "Me..." she says in a louder voice and a splayed hand on her chest, "and my friends..." she continues as she circles her arms to include the other three, "need to go here... To Rome..." She pokes the stick into the map she's drawn. "We need to go to Rome," she repeats and pokes the stick into the map as the man looks on.

"Why do you want to go to Rome?" comes a voice from behind Mary, startling her. She quickly turns around to see an elderly man in a tunic similar to Roman design. He has stark blue eyes and a white beard and Mary is still speechless. "You wish to go to Rome?" the man inquires again.

"Yes," Mary blurts. "You speak Greek?"

"Yes," the man says calmly. "Brennus sent word to me yesterday that you arrived in a boat with no sail and no rudder."

"Yes, that is correct, we are lucky to be alive," Mary sighs.

"This is Brennus, the chieftain of this village. My name here is Drust. My given name is Jeremiah."

"You are Jewish?" Mary asks astonished?

"Yes. You are only a small walk from Marseille. There is a Jewish community there."

"We thought we had landed a *long* way from Rome," Mary says with a smile.

"Oh, but you have," Jeremiah assures them. "But we can talk of that on the way. Do you have any belongings?"

"No, just what we're wearing," Mary says. "But we did have a companion that was with us, John. We have not seen him this morning."

Jeremiah asks a question of Brennus. After receiving an answer he says, "They have not seen your friend. They think he left during the night."

"Oh, I see," Mary says, "I hope he's alright."

"There are many large cities here, he'll run into one of them eventually," Jeremiah says. "So, let's be on our way... I've thanked Brennus for you. Just give him a bow as we leave."

Jeremiah bows a small bow and then turns to leave. Mary and the group follow suit and follow Jeremiah out of the village. In the light of day, a faint path can be seen but it is obvious that it is not well traveled. The group travels at a leisurely pace and Jeremiah strikes up the conversation again, "So, who are you and what are you doing here if you were headed to Rome?"

"Oh, where are our manners?" Mary says. "I am Mary Magdalene and this is my daughter, Sarah. This is Lazarus of Bethany and his sister, Martha. We came from Alexandria, but our galley sank in a great storm and we drifted here."

"And where exactly is 'here', by the way?" Lazarus asks.

"You are in the southern kingdom of Gaul" Jeremiah says. "It is the land on the border of the great sea that is at the end of the world."

"See," says Martha, "didn't I tell you?" Lazarus laughs.

"You past Rome to get here," Jeremiah continues. "Rome lies to the east, maybe five days travel by land."

"I've never heard of Gaul," Lazarus says. "Is it part of the Roman Empire?"

"Yes, but like most of the empire, not willingly," Jeremiah laments. "Gaul fell to the Romans a century ago. We are largely ignored as a loyal, but barbarian, holding. The provinces are run by local chieftains in a very stringent clan structure. But Roman influence has changed everyone here; the Celtic influence is being suppressed more every year."

"Celtic?" Lazarus asks.

"The Celts were here before the Romans came," Jeremiah explains. "They are the native people here. At least, as far as I know."

"So, how did Jews settle here?" Mary asks.

"We are the descendants of Jews who fled this direction from the last exile centuries ago." Jeremiah points ahead of him and says, "There. There is Marseille."

"That's a big city," Sarah says. "Why don't those people we were with come here to live?"

"There are still many tribes that choose to remain more primitive." Jeremiah says. "They continue to hunt and follow pagan gods and Druidic rituals. They speak a combination of Celtic and Latin."

"I'm not any good at Latin," Mary says.

"Me either," Lazarus echoes.

"That is the main language here. In the larger cities, they will speak some Greek too, but everyone here speaks Latin. Well... the locals like Brennus actually speak a rough combination of Celtic and Latin. There are many native languages here, all slightly different"

"I didn't think about that," Mary laments. "We're lucky we found you."

Apostle And Teacher

The group reaches Marseille and is warmly absorbed by the large Jewish community. No one living here has ever seen Jerusalem and the stories of Mary and Lazarus draw people from miles around. A couple of weeks later, Mary asks Lazarus to travel to Rome and see what Peter is up to. Martha stays behind with Mary and Sarah. As Mary speaks and begins to teach, often through an interpreter, she introduces them to the gospel of Jesus. Soon, she is teaching both Jew and Gentile and organizes several groups that begin to spread out over the land. Martha and Sarah also take an active part in the teaching and there is talk of organizing churches.

Two months pass and Mary is washing some dishes when the door to their modest home swings open. "It's me," Martha announces. "Are you ready?"

"Yes," Mary responds. Then turning to Sarah, "Martha and I are going to the market. Do you need anything?"

"Mama, say it in Latin," Sarah chides.

Mary heaves a heavy sigh and attempts to say, "I... and... Martha... go ...market." Sarah laughs. "What?" Mary asks.

"You just said that you and Martha are going to the *money*," Sarah giggles.

"Did I?" Mary says exasperatedly. "I *hate* Latin! Do you need anything or not?"

"No," Sarah giggles.

"Lets' go," Mary sighs as she heads out the door.

After they leave and are walking to the market, Martha says, "Sarah is getting pretty good with Latin."

"Yes, she is. I guess I would have tried harder if I knew we would be here this long. Still no word from Lazarus?" Mary asks although she already knows the answer.

"No. I'm ready to go to Rome myself and find him."

"Don't give up so easily. If there was something happening that we needed to know about, he'd have contacted us."

"Well, I'm ready to go home. This place is nice - and I can't believe I'm saying this - but I miss that hot, flea infested, dirt trap that I call home."

"If Lazarus doesn't show back up by the next full moon, we'll leave and go to Rome." Mary's thoughts quickly cycle, "Sara needs to find a man that will take care of her."

Martha laughs, "I think she enjoys being free... like her *mother*!"

"Oh Martha... Behave yourself. There just isn't anyone out there that can replace Jesus. Besides, you never remarried. That makes you free too."

"I have Lazarus to care for now," Martha sighs. "And he is two handfuls. I pity the woman who would marry that man." As they approach the market, Martha says, "You get the meat and spice. I'll get the vegetables." Mary nods and the women part ways to complete their shopping.

A week later finds Mary and Martha cooking supper together, as they do most nights. There is a sharp, hard rap on the door. Mary wipes her hands on her apron as Sarah is already opening the door. "Mama, it's Lazarus," Sarah announces. Martha drops her knife and bolts ahead of Mary wiping her hands on her own apron as well.

"Lazarus," Martha calls as she runs to hug him.

"Miss me?" Lazarus says with a grin.

"Only until I kill you myself," Martha exclaims anxiously. "What took you so long? Why didn't you contact us?"

"Calm down, sister. I'm here now," Lazarus assures her as Martha hugs him again. Lazarus inhales deeply as he smells the food cooking. "I'd love to tell you what has happened," Lazarus continues sarcastically, "but I think I'm just too weak from hunger. Perhaps after I've eaten something…"

"See?" Martha says exasperatedly. "Didn't I tell you? Pity!" Mary laughs as Martha storms back into the kitchen.

"Sit, Lazarus," Mary grins. "Rest your bones. Supper is almost ready. Sarah, wash up and then prepare the table please."

Supper is set out and the four, reunited once more, eat and talk. "So, it took me a while," Lazarus starts, "but I made it to Rome. The route along the coast goes up and around. It would have been much shorter by sail, but I don't think I'll ever get on a ship again."

"Is Rome as big as they say?" Sarah asks.

"Oh, child. All of the buildings are made out of smooth stone… mostly marble. The streets are even smooth and paved. There are statues everywhere. It's as if God carved the whole city out of one big mountain of marble."

"Wow!" Sarah says wide-eyed.

"Never mind the tour," Martha interrupts. "Did you find Peter?"

"Yes," Lazarus says. "It took me a while. The Master's followers are very secretive inside the city. They're scared, and with good reason. I had to gain a medium amount of trust before they would take me to Peter."

"Secretive?" Mary asks concerned. "Is it to protect themselves from persecution?"

"Yes. It was much worse than I expected."

"But Lazarus told me that you said the Romans ignored us," Martha says to Mary

"That is what I had heard," Mary explains.

"Well," Lazarus interrupts, "it was true until recently. Over the last year, even before Peter arrived, the level of persecution went up ten-fold. The new emperor blames them for everything that goes wrong. Now they are forced to meet in the catacombs under the city."

"What are catacombs?" Sarah asks.

"They are like tunnels," Lazarus explains. "They run under the whole city."

"So what is Peter doing now?" Mary asks.

"He is in hiding with them. Sarah, can you pass me more stew? He's trying to organize them and correcting all the falsehoods they've been told about Jesus; many spread by the Romans as a way to discourage the faithful."

"What do we do now?" Mary asks to no one in particular.

"We go home," Martha exclaims.

"I agree," Lazarus adds. "It is too dangerous in Rome right now and the *last* person Peter would be able to talk to is the emperor. Peter can probably make it out if he needs to, but there's nothing more there we can do."

"I can't leave now," Mary responds.

"Why not?" Sarah asks.

"There are so many here… The gospel is spreading here like a fire. I can't just leave them now."

"There are plenty of disciples to be made in Alexandria," Lazarus says. "Sarah would be safer there too."

"There is no danger here," Sarah chimes in. "Everyone like us."

"I like people here too," Martha says, "But it's time to go home – where we belong."

"Yes," Mary says halfheartedly, "maybe you're right. Maybe we do need to go back."

Lazarus and Martha make plans that evening to leave. Mary mopes and halfheartedly participates. Later that evening as they retire, Sarah whispers into the darkness, "You don't want to leave, do you?"

"Jesus told us to make disciples to the end of the earth," Mary whispers back. "That's here."

"Then you should stay. I'll stay with you."

"But I worry about you. Maybe we should go back. You need a husband."

"I know how important it is to spread this gospel which you've taught me. That's what is most important. Marriage can wait."

"For how long? And what about Matthew?" Mary says as she nudges Sarah.

"Well, some of the boys here aren't that bad either."

"They're... *exiled* Jews. You know, not *real* Jews," Mary says as she fumbles for words.

"I thought that's what we are now."

Mary smiles, "You're right. I guess we are, aren't we? Exiled by our own people." Mary sighs, "Go to sleep. We'll wait to morning to make a decision."

The night drags by as Mary tosses and turns. The argument continues in her head: Stay and make disciples or go and take Sarah back to a more stable environment. If persecutions are on the rise, the further they are from Rome, the safer for Sarah. But Jesus was never about being safe, and Sarah has come to understand that better than most. They are both the equivalent of 'dead' in the

Alexandria Jewish society. Safety only offers them an awkward attempt to reengage their lives. Mary asks for an answer from God, but is too anxious to hear it. Sleep finally overtakes her and the tussle is now confined to her dreams.

The next morning, Sarah and Martha are already fixing breakfast and Lazarus sits at the table when Mary enters. "Sorry, I slept late. I had a rough night."

"That's fine," Martha says.

"Sarah and I are staying," Mary says defiantly.

"Yes!" Sarah blurts out.

"Mary," Lazarus responds, "You can't guarantee your safety here."

"Life doesn't come with guarantees. You were dead, remember? We should all have been dead with the rest on that galley. We're living on borrowed time. We're living on God's time now." Mary walks to the window and opens the curtains to look out, "If this is where we are, then this is where God will use us."

"Well, then forgive me if I want to spend the rest of my borrowed time in my own bed," says Lazarus.

"There's nothing to forgive. You've done more than I would have ever dreamed to ask. Go home – both of you. We have disciples here. We'll be fine."

"I wish I could be so sure," laments Martha. "Is there nothing that I can say to bring you back home?"

"Forget it, Martha" Lazarus chuckles. "If I've learned anything about Mary, it's that her will is stronger than iron." Turning to Sarah as she approaches the table with his breakfast, he says, "Take care of your mother. She has the heart of a dove, but she has the head of a mule."

"You know if you stay, mama," Sarah giggles, "you'll *have* to learn Latin." Lazarus and Martha laugh in response.

"I know… I'll learn it – God help me… *please*," Mary pleads, which also garners laughter from the group.

That afternoon, Mary and Sarah wave to Lazarus and Martha as they begin the long trek back to Bethany. It is a sad good-bye, but one that all agree is for the best.

"Well," Mary says as she squeezes Sarah, "we're on our own again. Just you and me."

"We'll be fine," Sarah replies. "I'm not afraid of what is to come."

Mary smiles, "I never imagined that you would be my strength. I always had it figured the other way around."

Sarah laughs, "We are each other's strength."

The Miracle

"Go to the table and close your eyes," Mary says to Sarah from the kitchen.

"What?" Sarah asks confused.

"You heard me. Go sit at the table and close your eyes."

Sarah sighs, "Oh, alright." She puts her darning down and sits down at the table. She hears Mary walking up behind her. "What is going on?"

"It's a surprise. Keep your eyes closed." After a few moments, Mary says, "Open your eyes!" Sarah opens her eyes to behold the creation on the table in front of her.

Sarah asks in a tone of confusion, "A wedding veil?"

"Is it the wrong color? Do you like it?" Mary asks expectantly.

"Yes, it's beautiful. But I'm not getting married."

"Well, not yet. I'm just preparing…"

"Mama!" Sarah quips.

"Sarah, today is your fifteenth birthday. We've been here almost three years. You're just wasting away."

"Oh yeah, today *is* my birthday," Sarah says wistfully. "Two and a half years and I'm not wasting away," she says curtly.

"You're not getting any younger."

"Shira told me she didn't get married until she was almost seventeen."

"That was different. It wasn't because she didn't want to get married, there was just a lack of eligible men. And besides, God was saving her for a special purpose. She was meant to marry Matthias. You have plenty men here to choose from."

"How do you know God isn't saving me for a special purpose?"

"How do you know your special man isn't waiting for you right now?"

"I don't…"

"Then choose…"

"Mama!…"

Both of them stare at each other as the conversation lags into a stalemate. "Fine," Mary says with a sigh grabbing for the veil. "I'll put it up until it withers from dust… Like my daughter…"

In the years that pass after they arrive, Mary's renown within the region begins to spread out into the neighboring kingdoms. In the second year, a king from a neighboring clan brings his son to Mary to be healed. Although Mary is mostly known by the gospel story she witnesses to, she occasionally heals someone. The king is unimpressed with the stories he's heard, but is desperate to get his son healed. As Mary and Sarah gather eggs from their chickens into a basket outside their house, a small procession of armed men begins to trudge by. As they come to stop, Mary and Sarah are frozen in place not knowing what this harbinger brings. Then a man, more ornately adorned than the rest steps from the procession. He approaches Mary and boisterously declares, "I am King Bituitus of the kingdom Gallia Cisalpina." This means nothing to Mary, but she gives a little bow and tries to look impressed.

"Welcome to my humble home." Mary says.

"My son is sick. I've been told you possess great healing magic," Bituitus states.

70

"It is not magic. It is the power of my god."

"I care not about the source. I simply want my son healed. I have brought enough gold and spoils to make you a queen yourself – if you heal him," Bituitus motions to chests being off-loaded from a wagon.

"My god has no need of gold or wealth. That is not what he requires," Mary explains.

Bituitus appears stunned, "Then what exactly does your god demand of me?"

"Your allegiance to His kingdom," Mary says.

"What?" Bituitus says angrily. "I am a king, a Prince of Gaul. I owe allegiance to no one. Where is this kingdom you speak of?"

"Would you like to bring your son into the house?" Mary asks.

"No. Not until you've explained to me where this kingdom is and why I should pay such a heavy price."

"Come inside and let us sit and talk then," Mary turns to go into the house and motions Sarah to come as well.

They enter the house and Bituitus and two servants are seated at the table. Sarah sets the basket of eggs on the table and then rushes to bring them food and drink while Mary begins to explain who God is. She tells Bituitus of the love, charity and community of the church. She explains the heavenly kingdom of God and reads some of Isaiah. Hours pass as she tells stories of Jesus' ministry, death and resurrection. Bituitus rises from his chair as Mary reaches a lull.

"Do you really expect me to believe that this Jesus person was crucified and then came back to life?" Bituitus asks suspiciously.

"As surly as I am here before you," Mary attests.

"Ridiculous!" Bituitus insists. He points to the basket of eggs that Sarah sat on the table, "Those eggs would turn red before a man could come back to life…" His voice trails off. Before he can finish his last words, every egg in the basket begins to turn a deep crimson red. Within seconds, they are all completely changed. "That's… that's impossible…" Bituitus says shaken. "How did you do that?"

Mary, somewhat shaken herself, says, "I didn't." There is a solemn silence as everyone in the room stares at the eggs. Bituitus leans into the table and slowly reaches out for an egg. He touches one and then takes it into his large hand. He drops it down onto the table and it cracks open sending the pinkish egg white and a red yoke slowing crawling along the table top. Another pause while Bituitus wipes the side of his face with his hand. He turns to Mary and says, "I will give allegiance to this god, and more, if you will ask him to heal my son."

Mary closes her eyes a few moments and then says, "It is your very oath that has already healed your son."

Bituitus looks confused for a moment. He pulls back from the table and goes out the door. As he exits the house, he stops and sees his son walking towards the house lead by a servant from the wagon that carried his litter. As Mary comes to the door, Bituitus turns and kneels. "I give total allegiance and all that I have and all that I control to this living God." He looks up to Mary and says, "But I know nothing of him, except what you have told me. What must I do?"

"Go home. I will send helpers to you that will teach you and your people. You have nothing to fear, for God is good and kind."

Bituitus assembles his men and they leave to return home. He leaves a good portion of the money he had brought behind so Mary will be able to fund her ministry. Now, a year later, a knock comes to the door. "Tell me you did not invite a boy over here for me," Sarah says as Mary tucks away the veil into a small wooden box.

Mary grins, "I have no idea who that is." Sarah gives her a skeptical look as she rises to answer the door. "Really, I don't," Mary adds.

Sarah opens the door and the scraggly young man who stands there asks, "Is this the house of Mary?"

"Yes," Sarah replies. "What do you want?" Without a word, he simple holds out a rolled parchment. As soon as Sarah takes the parchment from his hand, he turns and begins to run away. "Thank you," Sarah calls after him, not knowing what else to say.

"Who was that?" Mary asks as Sarah closes the door.

"I don't know," Sarah responds looking at the item in her hand. "He just handed me this."

"Maybe it's a proposal," Mary teases as she reaches for the parchment.

"Mama…" Sarah whines as she rolls her eyes.

"I'm just kidding," Mary says as she sits at the table. "Who would be sending me a message? Especially one so official as to have a seal?" She breaks the wax seal which is still intact and unrolls the small parchment. "Whoever it is *obviously* doesn't know me very well – if they are assuming I can read this." She shows the parchment to Sarah.

"I can't read this either," Sarah explains.

"What? It's not Latin?"

"No. That's definitely not Latin," Sarah says as she hands the parchment back.

"Strange," Mary contemplates. "That means it could have come from anywhere."

The next day, Mary seeks out Jeremiah to see if he can tell her what this is. She hands him the parchment and he unrolls it and studies it for a few moments.

"No, I can't read this either," Jeremiah says. "It looks similar to the local language, but it's different. Which means it's probably from one of the neighboring kingdoms."

"I thought you told me all the kingdoms here used to be Celtic," Mary inquires.

"Yes," Jeremiah explains, "and that is why the language sounds the same most everywhere, but from what I've been told, each region developed their writing at different times. And since most of the people who can read or write only know how to in their own local language, it never changes."

"So, who can read this?" Mary asks.

"Let's go see a friend of mine. His name is Simon and he's the local scholar. He's traveled to most of the neighboring kingdoms."

The two of them make their way through Marseille to a small stone house set aside from the rest of the town. The vegetation around the house is overgrown and it looks from the outside as if the house is abandoned. "Simon lives here?" Mary asks.

"He's kind of odd, but he's got a brilliant mind," Jeremiah says reassuringly.

Jeremiah knocks on the door which is already slightly ajar, places his hand on it and swings it open. They enter into the house and stand just inside the door. Some dust dances in the sun beams coming through the high, un-shuttered windows and falling on a dusty wooden floor. The main room is filled with frail wooden tables stacked with tomes and parchments, some neatly and some strewn about. There is an eclectic collection of spears and shields and other things that Mary doesn't recognize scattered about the room; leaning against walls, standing in corners and laying on the floor. A middle-aged man with a long beard, unkempt appearance and stained tunic walks into the room seemingly unaware that he has visitors.

"Simon?" Jeremiah calls to him. He turns and notices them standing there.

"Jeremiah!" Simon calls out. He comes over and they hug. As he approaches, he has an aroma of someone long overdue for a bath. "You finally took my advice and got married, did you?"

"No, Simon. This is Mary… the disciple I was telling you about."

"Oh, yes. Welcome to my home… such as it is."

"Thank you," Mary says placing her hand to her nose as politely as possible.

"Simon," Jeremiah continues, "Mary has a parchment here and I can't read it. Can you?"

Jeremiah holds out the parchment and Simon takes it. He looks at it for a few seconds and, without a word, walks to a table and begins to dig through some other parchments. One by one, he studies a parchment retrieved from the stack and then, laying it aside, starts to dig again. After a soft "A-ha!" he drags over a tome on the table and, opening it up, begins to search through the pages. Mary and Jeremiah exchange glances. Simon then goes to another table to retrieve a quill and a small crucible that contains some kind of ink. He comes back to the open tome and begins scrawling notes in the border of one of the pages containing some writing and some illustrations.

"Simon?" Jeremiah interjects.

"Yes?" Simon responds.

"Can you read it? Do you know what it says?"

"Oh, sorry," Simon says setting the quill and ink aside. "Yes, although some words are unknown to me, so I was making note of them. And one of the words is used in a different way than I'm used to seeing it. I'm guessing at what those words mean based on context and the overall message. Well, they're also similar to other root words I've seen as well. Of course, if you examine the sentence structure…"

"Simon!" Jeremiah interrupts startling Simon. "What does it say?"

"Oh." Simon says nodding his head. "It appears to be an invitation, although strongly worded. And it bears the seal of King Vercingetorix, king of the Celtica clans."

"Invite? To what?" asks Mary.

"It does not say specifically," replies Simon. "It just says that you and your family are invited… or more likely, strongly encouraged… to be Vercingetorix's guest at a party… no, banquet, or maybe feast… that's one of the words I am not familiar with… ah… in your honor."

"A feast in my honor?" Mary says still confused. "What kind of feast? And why me?"

"Your name is known here throughout the clans of Vocontii," Jeremiah says. "We are one of the smaller clans; nothing really, compared to Celtica. But now that you have the allegiance of the kingdom of Gallia…"

"I only convinced the king to believe in God. I don't even know if he kept his word. I have no one in allegiance to me." Mary argues.

"Well," Simon says after a bit of reflection, "all the kings of this region have been at war with each other - at one time or another - since anyone can remember. All of them are agreed that the best way to defend ourselves against the Franks and to overthrow the Roman occupation is if all the kingdoms unite under a single king."

"That makes sense," Mary says.

"The only problem is, each king thinks it should be him." Simon sighs.

"That is a problem. So what does this king want with me?" Mary responds.

"They are constantly maneuvering to find any leverage over the others that they can use to advance their position," Simon explains. "Perhaps he sees you as leverage and wants to meet you before the others do."

"It is your name," Jeremiah says. "He sees you as either a potential enemy or a powerful ally, in case there is another major shift in power."

"So how do I know which one he thinks I am?"

"That will depend," Simon says, "on what you say when you accept his invitation."

"I would prefer not to go at all," Mary states.

"I agree," Jeremiah adds.

"Based on these two words here, I think it's more of a case where you go to see him before he comes to find you," Simon explains.

"I don't like this," Mary shakes her head. "I don't like this at all. It gives me a very bad feeling."

Friend Or Foe?

Hoping to ignore the request, Simon helps Mary craft a very polite message that is sent back to Vercingetorix saying that Mary has no transportation and that it is too perilous to easily travel that distance. Within the second week, an ornate coach appears at Mary's door and servants to help them in whatever they need. Mary decides that she should go now as opposed to waiting for armed soldiers to haul them away, so she and Sarah pack for the trip.

"Are you sure you want to come with me?" Mary asks Sarah

"Sure. You don't speak Latin as well as I do and you may need me. Besides, the invite said *family*," Sarah says with confidence.

"Thanks for your confidence in me," Mary replies sarcastically. "Well, it's not like you haven't been in danger before. I just worry about you."

"As long as we have Jesus, there is always hope," Sara says imitating Mary

Mary laughs, "Oh, very funny. But you're right... Or should I say, I'm right!"

The next morning the two are ushered into the coach and, with a crack of a whip, are whisked away on a new adventure. It is a five day journey that takes them through the heart of the Gaul region. It is a beautiful coach and shows a high level of craftsmanship. There are two plush seats that could hold two people comfortably facing each other. There are windows on both sides with a cloth shutter to block the direct sun if needed and framed with purple curtains which can be tied back. The ride is relatively smooth and they can each stretch out and recline sideways on the seats in order to catch a quick nap. The coach proves to be very comfortable and makes the journey less stressful. Mary notices how many heads it turns as they travel through a village. Mary chose early on not to venture very far beyond the city of Marseilles as the people always came to her. Now, Mary gets her first view of the world outside the city that she and Sarah have called home since they arrived. There are many small villages similar to the one where they landed. The majority of people appear to be very poor, but it's hard to tell from the brief images panning by. The empty stare from the locals as they glide by in such a luxurious coach makes Mary uncomfortable.

"I feel guilty riding in such luxury," Mary protests. "Did you see those people we just passed?"

"Yes," Sarah says shyly. "It's hard to look at them. Some of them look like they haven't eaten very much and here we are rolling by them in this."

"I had no idea it was this bad outside the main cities," Mary confesses. "I should have made myself go out and explore. See what the people needed."

"It's not your fault they have to live like this."

"No. But my Jesus would have been on the road looking to give comfort. So should I have been."

"So what do we do?" Sarah asks.

"There's nothing we can do now. But when we get home…" Mary says shaking her index finger in the air.

The first evening they stop, the servants set up tents and begin to cook. Mary and Sarah roll up their sleeves and begin to help.

"Can I cut up these potatoes for you?" Mary asks. The servants freeze and are speechless. This causes Mary and Sarah to stand motionless with confusion. Finally one of the women takes the knife from Mary's hand.

"Why would you help *us*?" the woman asks.

"Why not?" Sarah asks innocently.

"Because you are the royal guests of King Vercingetorix," the woman says. "Royal guests don't ever help servants."

Mary takes the knife back, "Oh, we're not that special. Let me help. I've been riding around all day, I've got to do something or I'll go crazy."

"Me too," Sarah giggles.

Reluctantly, the woman gives the potatoes back to Mary to cut up. Sarah is put to work making a sauce.

"Mama, I've never made a sauce like this before," Sarah says as she takes a small taste. "Oh, this is good. How do you make it?"

The woman smiles, "It's one of my mama's recipes. It's her special meat sauce. She says it's how she got my papa to marry her." Everyone laughs.

"Do you have some olive oil?" Mary asks. "I have a recipe that you would probably like."

"Not here," the woman replies sheepishly. "I have some back at the palace."

"Well maybe I can show it to you then," Mary smiles. The woman nods.

The servants are further distressed when Mary and Sarah prefer to sleep in the tents with them instead of in the coach.

"You really want to sleep in this dirty old tent? The bedrolls are not that comfortable," the woman complains.

"It hard for me to sleep sitting up," Mary explains. "Besides, after sleeping in that small boat, I don't think anywhere that is flat could be uncomfortable." Sarah laughs.

"I don't understand," the woman says puzzled.

"Never mind," Mary replies. "It's a long story." But Mary being Mary, she tells them her story and shares with them the gospel and begins to build bonds.

With each passing day, Mary sees more and more evidence of what the prolonged wars and the abject poverty have left as an inheritance to the children that stare at her with hollow eyes. Even Sarah becomes uncomfortable with the dichotomy of their situation and the people whom this king represents. Mary is determined to find a way to help these people, though she knows it will be heavily weighted by whatever this king wants of them. They stop to water the horses in a small village. Mary exits the coach followed by Sarah. Mary unwraps a cloth and takes the food left over from breakfast and begins to hand it out to the children gathered in curiosity.

"Takes this," Mary says as she hands a child a large piece of bread. The child slowly grabs it and then after a short pause, runs off. "We have to help these people," she says to Sarah.

Sarah takes some of the fruit and begins to pass it out also, "How do these children survive out here?"

The servants look on nervously. "What's wrong?" Mary asks.

"The king doesn't give his food away," one of the men mumbles.

"He doesn't sound like a very merciful man to me," Mary replies.

"No, my lady. He's not known to be," says the man. And then he hastily adds, "That's not to say he's a tyrant or anything like that. He's just not known to be… pleasant."

"His son," the woman interjects, "now he's friendly. At least to us servants."

"We'd better be getting on," the driver says. "If you ladies will get back in the coach…" Mary disperses the last portions of food. She shakes out the cloth and she and Sarah board the coach again.

On the afternoon of the fifth day, they come upon a large stone wall atop a large hill. It reminds Mary of Herodion, the hilltop fortress of King Herod. This parallel makes Mary even more anxious than she was before. She looks to see Sarah staring out the window and absorbed by the unfolding story that they are traveling through. "To be so innocent and full of life," Mary smiles inwardly. "She sits there unaware of how cruel this world can be. I am so afraid for us here. Whatever happens to us, I fear that she will be changed forever; unable to ever find that innocent child again."

They climb the hill and pass through the massive outer defensive wall. As soon as they pass through the gates, it's like passing through into another world. Left behind is the stark reality of poverty and hunger they have witnessed for nearly five days. In an instant, they are transported to an opulent dream world of beautiful buildings and beautiful people bustling through the streets. Sweet, perfumed aromas invades the coach. But the euphoric facade is broken quickly as the coach passes naked male and female slaves being auctioned off by a crier. Mary averts her eyes. Sarah is looking out the other side and doesn't notice.

The coach stops in front of what was probably a pristine white building at one time. The white has faded and it shows the scars of time and weather and war, but still holds a certain mystique of splendor. There is a wide staircase of cut stone steps that leads up to a heavy door and large iron censer-like bowls burn with fire on either side of the bottom step. There are many armed soldiers concentrated in this area and the crowds of people walking are much scarcer. The coach door swings open and a servant that Mary has come to know well helps her and Sarah out of the coach. The servant directs the two wayward travelers to the heavy wooden doors. As they climb the stairs, the doors stand open and have a great bar that lays across them, but it is set off to the side. A heavy-set guard waves them through the doorway at their approach and they enter.

The inside is even more opulent and is cluttered by carved marble statues and gold and bronze sculptures. They are quickly whisked to a large room with a large table in the middle surrounded by high-backed chairs. "Please, have a seat and wait here," one of the servants says as he retreats backwards out the door and it is closed, leaving the two of them standing alone in their silence.

"Wow," Sarah whispers. "I've never seen so many beautiful things in all my life."

"It is impressive," Mary whispers back as she moves to the table to take a seat. "I feel very under-dressed." Sarah begins to straighten her clothes after Mary's comment and she slowly walks to a table at the side of the room and reaches to touch one of the sculptures setting there. "Careful!" Mary admonishes, "We don't want to break anything."

"I'll be careful," Sarah says in an annoyed tone. "Sometimes, you treat me like I'm a little girl."

"I'm sorry," Mary says smiling, "I guess I haven't had a lot of experience being a mother."

It is now late in the day and the sun streams through a big window and makes an elongated image on the patterned rugs. The window is framed in a lush, purple fabric which is gathered on either side by silken cords. There are silver serving flasks and bowls in the center of the table, though they look as if they have not seen use in some time. There are carved wooden panels along the walls that show a high degree of workmanship. There is a cracking sound and the doors fly open and attendants flow into the room and stand in readiness. Mary stands up and Sarah quickly darts from her exploring to stand at Mary's side. After a few moments, a man in a purple robe tied with a black sash enters the room. He is adorned with jewelry including several large rings and a heavy necklace that boasts a large stone at the end. As he passes, all the attendants bow.

"Welcome," The man blurts out with elevated hands as he enters the room. "I hope your trip was not too tedious."

"No," Mary responds, "it was quite comfortable. Thank you for the coach."

"My pleasure," the man responds. "Please, sit and we will get acquainted." He quickly sits in the chair at the end of the table and motions for the two of them to sit on either side. "I am King Vercingetorix, ruler of all Celtica and Prince of Gaul," he says as the women sit.

"Pleased to meet you," Sarah says dutifully.

"Yes, we are honored to be here," Mary adds.

"No, it is I who am honored to have you accept my invitation," Vercingetorix says. "So... You are Mary Magdalene?"

"Yes," Mary responds. "I am Mary and this is my daughter Sarah. I must say, I am still puzzled as to why you invited us."

"Ah, invited indeed," Vercingetorix muses. "Well, as I understand it, you are the wife of this *Jesus* person I hear my subjects talking about. You are the one whom he loved."

"You could say that in a way…," Mary hesitates.

"And I also understand," Vercingetorix interrupts, "that this Jesus is '*King* of the Jews'?"

"I need to explain that. You see, he is what the Jews call, the Messiah. He is the only son of the Hebrew God, but when…"

"And so he is royalty! Son of a god!" Vercingetorix interrupts again with a large smile. "And it is my business to know all the royalty in Gaul."

"But you need to know the whole story," Mary states.

"And I will," Vercingetorix says in an assuring tone. "But you're probably ready to clean up for dinner and get out of those horrid traveling clothes." He stands and claps his hands loudly. The doors fly open once more and there is another incoming stream of servants. "Show these women to their room," he commands. He then turns back to Mary, "We will talk more at dinner and you can tell me the whole story." He then exits the room swiftly followed by the same stream of servants. The two left behind motion to Mary and Sarah to follow them.

Mary and Sarah are met in their room by a handful of female servants who begin to wait on them. They are seated in two large, plush chairs with a small table between them. One woman hands each of them a large goblet of wine and another places a tray of assorted fruits on the table between them. Sarah is somewhat anxious at all the attention buzzing around her. However, Mary seems to unconsciously slip into an old familiarity and appears to Sarah to be quite at home.

"Mmmm," Mary moans as she sips the wine. "This is real wine, Sarah. Not like the watery stuff we have. Don't drink this stuff too quickly."

Sarah takes a sip. Her eyes get big and all she can say is, "Wow."

Other women now bring stools and, without a word, pick up both women's feet and slide the stool underneath. Soon they are massaging the feet to a chorus of moans and groans.

"Oh, it's been a long time since I was pampered like this," Mary coos.

"It's strange," Sarah moans, "but I like it."

Mary laughs, "Enjoy it while it lasts, because it won't last long." One of the women asks a question, but Mary is unable to understand it. "I'm sorry," she says, "but I didn't understand a word you said."

"She asked if you wish to bathe now," one of the other women says in Latin.

"Oh, that would be nice," Mary says drowsily. The woman begins to give orders to the others and soon they are pouring water into a tub.

"Your bath is ready, my lady," the one woman says.

"Thank you," Mary responds. She gets up and walks over to the tub and begins to remove her clothes.

"Are you going to bathe in front of all of these strange women?" Sarah asks as she begins to blush and fidget.

"It's not a big deal," Mary says as she steps into the tub and slides below the water. "Just relax and enjoy it."

"I don't know about that," Sarah says nervously. There is a small pitcher of water that is poured over Mary's head. One woman begins to scrub her back while another begins to wash her hair.

The one woman then addresses Sarah, "If you wish to undress, you can put on this wrap while we wash your clothes."

"Yes, do it Sarah," Mary calls from the tub. Sarah reluctantly undresses and surrenders her clothes to the woman. She quickly wraps herself in the cloth as best she can and shrinks back down into the chair. After Mary steps from the tub, she is dried and wrapped in a long piece of cloth like Sarah is wearing. "Well? Come on," Mary says impatiently and motioning to Sarah to come to the tub. Sarah makes her way nervously to Mary. Mary says, "Oh, don't be such a baby," as she begins to unwrap Sarah's cloth. Sarah steps into the tub and almost slips into falling. Once seated, the women come with another pitcher and begin to repeat the same procedure.

"Well?" Mary inquires after a few minutes. "What do you think?"

"I think I've died and gone to heaven," Sarah coos.

Mary laughs, "Yes, it can be addicting." Sarah lightly moans.

The two of them sit in the plush chairs, sipping wine in their cloth wraps.

"King Vercingetorix talks a lot," Sarah says.

"He does," Mary responds while reaching for some fruit. "He wears me out just listening to him... 'horrid traveling clothes'? He's going to be disappointed when he finds out that those were our good clothes."

"Why does he think you're Jesus' wife? Are you?"

"Yes, in a way... It complicated," Mary responds hesitantly. "But he is convinced that we are some kind of Jewish royalty."

"What are we going to do now?"

"I don't know. I will have to tell him the truth, if he will hear it. I won't lie to you Sarah, I'm afraid for us when I tell him we're not royalty."

"What will he do?" Sarah asks with a fearful voice.

"I don't know. He may just kick us out. But I sense he wants something from us... from me."

"What?"

"I don't know that either. But, listen to me... listen to me very carefully. It may be safer for us if we *ease* into the fact that we're not royalty. We'll play along for now... And if anybody asks, you are my daughter from birth, understand? No one is to know you're adopted – *no one*!" Sarah nods. "I will tell him at the appropriate time. But, I want to find out what he's up to first."

"Up to?" Sarah asks quizzically.

"He asked us here for a reason. It wasn't just because he thinks we're important. We have something he wants; I can just feel it. I just need to find out what it is." Sarah nods again. "Just follow my lead and do what I do and don't tell Vercingetorix or anybody else anything about what we've been doing just yet. I think it'll be safer that way."

Shortly before dusk, Mary and Sarah's clothes are returned to them, cleaned and slightly perfumed. Mary opens the chest they brought with them and starts going through their clothes. She picks out the best of their dresses and asks the servant if these dresses can be perfumed like the clothes that were returned. The servant complies with Mary's request. The two women dress and prepare to meet Vercingetorix for the evening meal. A servant enters and motions them to the door. They follow and are walking down a wide hallway. "It's going to be strange," Sarah muses, "eating food that I didn't cook myself."

Mary smiles, "Don't get used to *that* either." Sarah laughs. They are escorted into a large dining hall. Vercingetorix is already seated at the head of a long table and they are to sit to his right side. There are several women seated down the left side of the table. As they are being seated, a young man Sarah's age appears and helps her with her chair. As Sarah sits, she turns to thank him, but only gets part of it said. She stares at him as she sits and he seems to be frozen in place staring at her. He is a handsome young man with piercing hazel-like eyes and burgundy-red hair which falls on his shoulders in twisting curls at the end. He has a rugged chin covered with a thin beard and exudes an air that spellbinds Sarah as her stare starts to become a gawk. When Mary notices them, she lightly elbows Sarah breaking the spell between them. The young man quickly sits next to Sarah and they both sit lost in their temporary embarrassment; glancing at each other but trying to look like they are not. Soon the table fills with younger children and old men. It is difficult to see everyone because of the length of the table and centerpieces which block the line of sight.

"Welcome to my honored guests," Vercingetorix thunders. "Let us eat!" he announces while slapping his hand together loudly. At once there is a quickly-becoming-familiar stream of servants marching like ants to and from the table bringing all types of food and placing it in front of the people seated.

"I've never seen some of this food," Sarah whispers discretely. "Can we eat it?"

"Of course," Mary whispers sweetly back. "Try it. If you like it, then eat it."

Once the majority of servants depart, the few that remain walk around the table dishing up food to the participants. Vercingetorix's table manners leave much to be desired, but Mary has seen worse.

"So, we are gathered tonight," Vercingetorix says boisterously, "to honor my guest Mary Magdalene and her daughter Sarah." He motions to the young lad seated next to Sarah, "This is my eldest son, Prince Litaviccos." Sarah can feel her face blush as she looks at him. Vercingetorix motions to the opposite side of the table from Mary, "And these are all of my wives."

"All of them?!" Sarah blurts out bringing about a harder elbowing from Mary. "I mean... ah, sorry."

Vercingetorix laughs and then asks confused, "I though Jews also kept many wives?"

"It is an old custom," Mary explains. "A few do, but not so much anymore."

"Ah... After listening to them argue among themselves for days, I can see the wisdom of that decision," Vercingetorix says as he receives glares from most of the women on the other side of the table. "And these are all my children," he says motioning down the table. "And at the end are my advisors."

There is some small talk between Mary, Vercingetorix and the wives directly across from Mary. Sarah manages the courage to give Litaviccos a proper thank you for assisting her to sit.

"So, tell me," Vercingetorix says, "I want to know about this Jesus person. He was the Jewish king before the Romans killed him?"

"Well... yes and no..." Mary hesitates.

"Yes and no?" asks Vercingetorix. "The Romans called him out as king, did they not?"

90

"The Romans were the ones who nailed him to the cross. They put a sign above his head that read, 'King of the Jews' to mock him."

"So, he was not a king?"

"He is the Messiah, who is a heavenly king," Mary continues. "His kingdom is not of this earth. His kingdom is a heavenly kingdom where he rules with our God over all of creation."

"If he is God's son, then why did your God not save him?"

"He did not come into this world to rule it. He came to sacrifice himself for the world that it might be saved into God's kingdom."

"So what are you planning to do here? In Gaul?"

"Jesus commanded us to make disciples in all the world to further God's love and compassion. But in truth, I was also forced to leave Judah for fear of my life."

"Because of your relationship to Jesus, the king?"

"Yes, you could say that I and Sarah are in exile here."

"I cannot allow you to take over my subjects to serve your God," Vercingetorix explains.

"No," Mary explains, "as I said, his kingdom is not of this earth. Your subjects will remain you subjects. By taking Jesus as their savior, they may enter into God's kingdom when their lives here are spent."

"Ah, I think I see now," Vercingetorix says. "I am happy to hear that. You intrigue me with this story and I want to hear more… and now I don't have to kill you and your daughter as conspirators."

"That is very good news," Mary says with a large sigh. "Let me start at the beginning…"

Planting The Seeds

Mary and Sarah stay at Vercingetorix's palace another three weeks. Mary tells Vercingetorix many of the stories of Jesus and Vercingetorix makes plans to assist Mary in helping the people throughout the region. Sarah and Litaviccos also spend time walking and talking together in the gardens. Vercingetorix seems to show little interest in helping the subjects he rules, but he is very interested in Mary helping them. It is a contradiction that leaves her scratching her head. Sarah comes through the door and, with a long, pleasant sigh, hands a parasol-like shade to one of the servants.

"Another walk with Litaviccos?" Mary inquires as she sews.

"Yes," Sarah sighs dreamily. "Vio and I were discussing flowers."

"Vio?" Mary says slyly.

"Oh, that's what his mother calls him. So I asked and he said I could call him that as well."

"I see," Mary muses. "And you two were discussing flower?"

"Yes…"

"In the garden?"

"Yes…"

"Alone?"

"Mama!"

Mary Laughs. Sarah comes and sits next to Mary with a beaming smile, "Vio loves flowers. He's planted most of the gardens himself. He enjoys planting. He says it takes his mind off his problems."

"What problems?" Mary probes.

"Oh, he didn't say. Just whatever problems come up, I guess."

"Are you two getting serious?" Mary teases.

"Maybe," Sarah says hesitantly.

"You know how many wives Vercingetorix has. Do you want to be just one in the crowd of Litaviccos' wives?"

"I don't know," Sarah says as her smile vanishes. Sometimes it bothers me, but other times I don't really care."

"What? You can't be serious."

"I don't want to talk about it right now," Sarah says defensively.

"I'm sorry, but we do need to talk about it. You are Jewish and Litaviccos is not. I don't trust Vercingetorix or Litaviccos."

"Why?" snaps Sarah. "Vercingetorix is helping you make disciples. What's not to trust?"

"He's not interested in his people. He's not interested in my results. He's only interested in my efforts for some reason."

"I don't understand."

"Neither do I. When I've asked him about building churches and organizing the disciples we already have, he's not interested. He just wants me to reach further and further out into the region. He even wants me to go outside the area he controls. He wants everyone in Gaul to hear the gospel," Mary rants.

"What are you complaining about? That sounds like good news to me."

"He's being too helpful; too aggressive. I don't trust him," Mary mutters

93

"Well, I trust Vio. He's never been anything except nice to me. And I don't care if he's not Jewish," Sarah says as she storms into the next room. Mary drops her head and sighs.

True to his word, Vercingetorix begins sending Mary further and further away from the palace. Sarah goes with her at first, but soon Mary is gone for weeks at a time and Sarah cannot handle the conditions. But the poor conditions that exist are a constant reminder to Mary of her calling and of the mission. She worries that she has lost her ministry companion to a palace lifestyle of pampering and plenty.

Mary always brings food and supplies to share with the poor. And there are always plenty of them that show up to hear the stories of Jesus. They bring their sick to be healed and to take away hope that their pain is not all that they have. They come from leagues away and the constant crowds and the teaching and the healings begin to weigh Mary down in the same way the crowds that gathered around Jesus did. There are a few brave souls which band with her and become her disciples to help with the constant work and the loading and unloading of the pack animals.

Mary returns after an exhausting trip which takes her to the outer-most region of Gaul. She is struggling to walk and news of her condition precedes her to the palace. Sarah stands at the gate awaiting her arrival. When she sees Mary, her breath is stolen away. Mary walks in an almost trance as she seems content just to put one foot in front of the other. There is a man on either side of her to hold her upright. Sarah run to her and takes hold of her arm from one of the men, "Mama? Mama, speak to me," she says is a panicked voice.

"I'll make it," Mary mumbles. She has a vacant stare. Sarah places her hand to Mary's face and feels a fever.

"She's burning up," Sarah says. Turning to the man who was holding her up, "Why is she still walking?"

"She refused to ride or take our help, Lady Sarah," the young disciple says.

Sarah gets Mary into her bed and begins to care for her. Mary sleeps through the next day, but in the afternoon of the second day wakes to see Sarah sitting by her side.

Sarah springs from her chair, "You're awake!"

Mary coughs. Then she says, "Of course I'm awake. What time is it? It's late. I have to get up."

Sarah pushes her back down into the bed, "You still have a fever. You're not going anywhere until you're better."

"I overslept. No big deal," Mary says between coughs.

"You've been asleep for almost two days!" Sarah quips as she gets Mary to drink some water.

"I have?" Mary says astonished. Sarah nods. "Well, maybe I'm a little ill."

"You scared me. What happened to you out there?"

"I don't know. I started feeling bad just as we were headed here. It will probably go away in a day or two."

"Until then," Sarah says sternly, "you are not getting out of bed."

Morning comes and Mary breezes into the kitchen area from the bedroom. "How are you feeling today?" Sarah asks.

"I feel good. I think I'm ready to get back out there," Mary says confidently.

"It took you two weeks to recover," Sarah reminds her while seated at the table and eating breakfast, "maybe you should take a longer break. I'm worried about you."

"I'm worried about you," Mary quips back.

"Me?"

"Yes, you."

"Why would you be worried about me? I'm feeling fine. I really like it here," Sarah announces.

Mary stoops in front of Sarah to look her in the eye, "That's why I'm worried."

"I don't understand," Sarah says perplexed.

"I'm worried about who you are becoming... who you have become," Mary says as she shoos one of the servants away to gather her own breakfast. Sarah just stares. "I've watched you these past two weeks while I was recovering."

"I'm still lost."

Mary sits with her food, "You order these servants around like you own them. You look down at them now. Are you so much better than they are?"

"I do?"

"Yes. You have been beguiled into a life of luxury. When was the last time you ate your own cooking? When was the last time you made your own bed or did your own laundry? When you came here, you thought it strange to let others wait on you. Now you've come to expect it."

"I'm sorry," Sarah says as she hangs her head. "You're right. What was I thinking? I'm sorry, I was not aware I was doing that. I certainly don't think I'm better than anyone else here."

Mary reaches out and lays her hand aside of Sarah's head, "It's easy to do. I know. Trust me when I say I speak from experience. You've lost your way... we both have. You let yourself get lost here and I let myself get lost out there."

"How did you get lost?"

"I was trying to save the world, and I can't. Jesus showed me how to lead out in front, but I was in the back trying to push."

"So what are you going to do now?"

"I'm going to do what I do best. Organize!" Mary beams. "It's time to build some churches whether Vercingetorix is ready or not." Sarah's face turns sad as she looks away. "What's wrong, Sarah?"

"I have forsaken my God. You are right, I did lose myself here."

"There is always forgiveness," Mary says.

"I will come with you. It is my turn to serve again, although…" Sarah's voice trails off.

"It will mean leaving Litaviccos," Mary says. Sarah nods. Mary lays her hand on Sarah's, "It will be hard for you. But God will provide for you when the time is right. Trust in that. Besides, it's not like you won't ever see him again… just not every day."

THE LEGEND IS BORN

In four years, Mary starts five churches. One is newly started and has no place to meet yet. They meet where they can and when they can, but there are always people coming for healing, food and hope. Two of the churches have built structures which amount to pavilions. They do little for wind and dust and cold, but they do keep the congregation's heads dry if it's raining. One of the churches has a cloth structure which looks like the tabernacle used by the wandering Jews in the exodus. The last church, which is outside of the region of Celtica, is small and meets in a structure eclectically pieced together using timbers, various stone, tree bark and mud bricks. Mary and Sarah regularly make rounds between the five, sometimes together and sometimes separately. At each visit, stories are corrected, healing is performed and food is distributed. Mary's name and reputation floods the neighboring regions and many, both rich and poor, are beginning to believe.

"Sarah," Mary calls as she sits sewing, "Will you bring me my basket?" Sarah appears from the kitchen and grabs a small basket full of sewing things and brings it to Mary. "Thank you, dear," Mary says with a smile. There is a loud rap on the door of the small house where they are temporarily staying. They exchange glances as Sarah goes to open the door. A man bursts through the open doorway. He is a member of the church where they are staying and one of the leaders that Mary has trained. He was a Frank that was orphaned when he was young and was raised by a Jewish family in the area. The look on his face told Mary this was not going to be a business as usual day. "Isaac, what's wrong?" Mary implores.

"Mary!" Isaac says trying to catch his breath. "To the north... many people dead... they say the hand of our God reached down from the heavens and killed them. It also destroyed much of the town. They are blaming you and the followers that are there. You must come!"

"Sarah, we must pack quickly," Mary says flustered. "Let us go see what has happened. Quickly!"

Three days brings them to the doorstep of the village. All during the journey, they hear stories of death and destruction, but every story is different. Mary and Sarah are now standing confused and dazed as they stare at the devastation. The whole city seems to have been leveled to the ground and all that remains are piles of mud bricks and timbers.

"I have never seen anything like this in my whole life," Mary whispers with her hand to her face.

"It looks like a war happened here," Sarah responds.

"This looks like more damage than even men are capable of," Mary says as she begins to walk the main road still cluttered with debris. As they walk, they pass families digging and sifting through piles of what is left. There is some crying, but the mood seems to be more somber, yet resolute, as people try to put their lives back together. Small fires burn almost everywhere with old women and children huddled around them. Mary stops at one of the fires where a woman tries to comfort her crying children and there is no pot on to cook. Mary unpacks some food and gives it to the woman, "For your children." The woman manages a numb smile and nods as Mary and Sarah continue on their way. They finally make eye contact with someone they know. "John," Mary speaks with tears as she hugs the man, "what happened here?"

John moves to a small patch of rocks where they can sit. It has been days, but John still looks lost and confused. He speaks in a hushed tone and his voice still trembles. "I have never seen anything like it in my life. And I never want to see it again in my lifetime, God forbid."

"What was it?" Mary asks.

"It was the hand of God," John says in awe.

"Tell me everything you saw," Mary says as she takes John's hand.

John speaks with a glazed look and monotone voice, "It was about mid-day I guess. There was a heavy storm, but it was just like most winters. Then some of us saw it." John points his index finger towards the ground and starts to wiggle it back and forth as he speaks. "Like a long, black finger at first; it poked through the clouds and came down and started to rub along the ground. It looked like it was a long way off. But as it got closer, it began to get bigger. It looked like a big fist maybe." John looks away up the littered road.

"Go on, John. What happened then?" Mary urges him on.

"It made a thunderous noise as it got closer. The fist grew and grew until it seemed to cover the whole horizon. It was picking up things... large things... tree tops and roofs and tossing them aside. It just kept coming and coming and coming..." John's voice trails off.

"John," Mary says patting his hand and grabbing his arm. It breaks him out of his stare and turns his face back to her. "It's ok. It's ok, John." She reassures him.

"Some people ran. Others went into their houses and closed all the shutters. It didn't matter. A lot of those who ran were found dead… some leagues down the road. It picked them up like dolls. Those who hid were mostly buried in their houses as the great fist toppled them over like they were grass. I was lucky, I guess. It tossed me out of my house and I landed with a load of timbers and bark. Some of the timbers fell on me and I got this gash," John points to a large cut on the side of his forehead. "Thought they broke my leg too, but they didn't."

"Where's Ruth, John?" Mary asks. "Where's Ruth?"

"Dead," John says with little change in emotion. "She was killed when the wall fell in on her. Buried her yesterday with some others."

"I'm so sorry, John," Mary says as she hugs him again.

"Why?" John asks. Mary says nothing. "Why did God take so many of us?"

"I don't know," Mary shakes her head and sobs. "I just don't know."

They get John to his feet and he walks with them to the center of town. They pass a couple of other believers that join them in tears and hugs and walk with them. As they reach the center of town, there is a crowd of people milling around. In the center of the street, there is a crude, elevated, wooden table meant to serve as some type of altar. Upon it is the body of the town elder. She appears to be dead. At the base of the table are the beginnings of a bonfire.

One in the crowd recognizes Mary and the relative silence is broken with, "There she is!" This gets everyone's attention and suddenly Mary feels the whole town staring at her. "It was her and her God that brought the destruction upon us!" The woman walks towards Mary and the crowd begins to coalesce. As they approach the mummers become louder.

"Mama?" Sarah says, "What now?"

"There is always hope," Mary states. "God is good."

As the crowd closes in, John steps in front of Mary and holds up his hands. "Stop!" he commands and the crowds falls silent. "You know me. You know Ruth. You know what kind of man I used to be. You know what kind of a man I've become since this God found me. I was just reminded that this God brought me hope when there was none. He showed me compassion when I needed it. This God showed me love when my heart raged with evil." He motions to Mary, "You want to hold this woman responsible for deaths she did not commit with her own hand? My great-grandfather was born here and I've been told since that time, and remember a good bit of it myself, that we've done a fair job of killing each other with *our* own hands. I lost my wife... but I do not blame that on this woman. Instead of wandering around half dead, today I will give thanks for my own life and those of us that are still here."

"Thank you, John," Mary says. "Who is this woman?" she asks pointing to the altar table.

"She is Esselt, the town elder," comes a voice form the crowd. "She is the oldest daughter of the dead chieftain."

"When the last chieftain died," John explains, "there were no sons. So, she was appointed elder until another chieftain was selected. She was not a believer, but you wouldn't know it. She led with a wise and compassionate heart."

Mary begins to walk towards the table cutting a large swath through the crowd. She stops near the table and lifts up her hands. "Oh Father," she says in a loud voice, "This was a just woman in the eyes of these people. Send her back that she might lead in your ways. That through her, these people will become a mighty army for you and live for your glory." Mary then points to the woman and cries, "Wake up, Esselt. Come back to us and rule once more."

There is hush over the entire square broken only by the sounds of nature in the distance. Time seems to stop as seconds creep by. As the tension begins to break and people start to exhale and the murmurs begin, Esselt's eyes pop open and she begins to raise her head. The crowd releases a collective gasp. Some grow weak or faint away. Some take off running in different directions to bring news to the rest of the village. Most, including Sarah and John, are frozen in place. After Esselt sits up, she swings her legs over the edge of the table and sits looking around. While most are still stunned, a couple of men come forward to help her down. Some in the crowd begin to cry and some are frightened presuming her to be a ghost.

Esselt walks to Mary and reaches for her hand. "Mary Magdalene," Esselt says with familiarity.

"You know me?" Mary asked puzzled.

"I know you, Mary," Esselt smiles. "You are the favored disciple of Jesus. I know your whole life."

"How do you know me?"

Esselt leans into Mary and whispers, "I've been to the other side, dear. We need to talk." But before Mary can say a word, Esselt holds up her hand to silence Mary. "Later..." she nods and winks. She then walks around the table that she had spent days occupying in a wide circle to view the crowd that has gathered. There are those in the crowd that are frightened and cower as she comes near. She stops and tries to offer words of comfort. She finally addresses the crowd, "My friends, I have seen death. I have much to share with you."

Less than an hour later, the entire village turns out. Esselt now stands on the table that was her death bed and tells her story. "My friends, I have been to the other side of death. I cannot tell you everything because my words fall short. I wandered in the dark for so long. It was cold and miserable and without form. Then, when Mary spoke to her God... to *my* God... I was thrust into the light. Many things were made clear to me. It took a long time, but also no time at all." Many in the crowd begin to stare in puzzled looks. "I know it sounds crazy, but it's not. But most important of all, I return to you with the word of eternal life; that none need to walk in the darkness I was in." Mary and Sarah sit in the crowd and listen to Esselt as she goes on to speak of the love and compassion of God. She speaks of Jesus so intimately, as if she had known him her whole life. It takes Mary back to the shores of the Sea of Galilee when Jesus spoke to the crowds of Jews that would gather everywhere he went. After Esselt finishes, the crowd disperses with smiles and hope replaces the despair. Esselt organizes the rebuilding effort and the first four months show an amazing metamorphosis.

Some weeks later, Esselt finds Mary planting a small sapling near one of the recently rebuilt homes. "Mary?" Esselt says as she walks up. "You have not come to talk with me."

"I've been so busy," Mary says not looking up. "You've been so busy."

"You have not come because you are scared," Esselt says softly.

Mary ceases her planting and hangs her head with a heavy sigh. "I *am* scared," she admits. Esselt grabs Mary's arm and helps her up. She pulls Mary over to a bench and they both sit.

"You are scared, but you don't know what you're scared of," Esselt explains.

"I was afraid you brought bad news to me," Mary says. "I believed God was angry with me for some reason."

"It is true that Jesus warned you not to come here," Esselt says in a pleasant voice. "But you, of all people, should know that there is always grace and forgiveness." Mary nods. "But now that you are here, you cannot leave. You cannot go back to Alexandria."

"What?" Mary asked shocked. "Why?"

"Too many things have happened. There is too much in motion. It is hard to explain, but God's plan is always advancing and always in motion. I can only tell you that your life is in danger, but know that God has already taken care of it."

"I don't understand."

"Yes, I know. And I wish I could help you to understand."

"So what will happen to me? What will happen to Sarah?" Mary asks panicked.

"I do not know," Esselt responds.

"But you know me. You know my life. You know I'm in danger…"

"I know your past," Esselt says trying to calm Mary. "God revealed it to me. But I am not God. I do not know what lies ahead… not even for my own life."

"So what do I do now?" Mary asks in a lost voice.

"You have led a remarkable life." Esselt says placing her hand to Mary's cheek. "Keep living your life. Follow your heart knowing that you are favored by God and that he still rejoices in your service and is watching over you. But most of all, be true to your love, Jesus." Mary nods and the two exchange smiles.   Esselt leaves Mary to return to her planting, but Mary sits lost in thought.

On The Run

Esselt's words continue to haut Mary. She is more worried for Sarah than for herself. She wrestles with the many questions in her head. Is Sarah's life in danger too? Should she tell Sarah what Esselt told her? How would she keep it from Sarah? She returns that evening to the place where they are staying while the village is being rebuilt. She is uneasy and quickly distracted. Sarah can see it which makes her uneasy as well.

Sarah asks, "What's wrong, mama? Tell me."

"What makes you think something is wrong?" Mary asks in a caviler tone.

"Maybe because you've had that needle poking through the same hole since yesterday," Sarah says irritated.

Mary glances down and realizes she hasn't gotten any sewing done. "Oh," is all Mary can manage.

"Please tell me what is wrong." Sarah begs.

"You're right. You're too old for me to be hiding things from you. And, I guess it affects you as well," Mary says in exasperation.

"What is it?"

"Esselt. She told me my life was in danger."

Sarah just stares. After a moment she says, "And…."

"And? We could be killed any moment," Mary exclaims.

"I thought it was something serious," Sarah says with a teasing sneer.

"Serious? What?.." Mary sees the mischievous grin on Sarah's face and exhales deeply. She looks again and the

107

expression on Sarah's face makes the grin contagious. Mary can feel the tension in herself break and she too begins to grin. "It is serious," Mary chuckles.

"What are you going to do?"

"I don't know. But it's driving me crazy just sitting around waiting for something to happen."

"Did Esselt say we would die?" Sarah quizzes.

"Well... no, not really. She just said 'danger' actually."

"And you assumed she meant death."

"Yes, you're right. Maybe I am making a bigger deal out of this than it should be."

"Maybe you're just going to fall and break both your legs," Sarah giggles. "Something simple."

"You're very reassuring," Mary rolls her eyes.

"What can we do?"

"Maybe the best thing to do is keep moving. If we don't stay in any one place to long, maybe we can stay ahead of whatever it is."

"Or maybe we walk into it if we leave here."

Mary lays her sewing down, gets up and walks over to Sarah. She places her gentle hand on Sarah's cheek and says sweetly, "You're really not helping here, sweetie!" Sarah chuckles.

Finally Mary realizes that there is nothing to be done and that whatever comes will come and she will have to deal with it then. She and Sarah stay in the village to finish planting the fields. All the destroyed homes have been rebuilt for those families that survived; some better than before. The fields are the last piece needed for the villagers to begin providing for themselves once more. Another week and Mary and Sarah will be on their way.

It is almost dusk and Sarah is finishing dinner. They plan on leaving to go back home either tomorrow or the day after. "I just ran out of olive oil," Sarah laments. "I need just a small bowl. I'll go see if I can borrow some."

"No, you finish up," Mary insists. "I'll go borrow some." Mary slips out the door before Sarah can argue. Mary leaves the door ajar as she will be right back. She knocks on the door of a neighboring house and an old woman pokes her head out the door. "We just ran out of oil. Can I borrow a small bowl?" Before the woman can answer, they are both distracted by horseman riding hard into town. Mary pushes her way into the doorway so that she is barely visible. "Those are Roman soldiers," she mumbles. The men stop and dismount. They run and fling open the door to Mary's house and run inside. Mary covers her mouth with her hand as she gasps and finishes pushing her way in the door.

"Roman soldiers? Here?" the old woman exclaims.

"They ran into my place," Mary says alarmed.

"Poor Sarah! What will they do to her?" the old woman asks.

"I don't know," Mary says as her mind is racing and panic is building in the room. "They must be after me. This is what Esselt meant." Then turning to the old woman pleads, "You have to hide me. Quickly!"

"I have nowhere to hide you," the old woman says panicky. "Jacob," she says to her husband, "take her out the back door. Quickly."

Mary follows the old man out the back door and down the small street behind the houses. The old woman goes to the door and opens it. She sees the soldiers coming out of Mary's house and quickly closes the door. The old man knocks on a door and it opens. "Romans! Hide her!" is all the old man gets out while shoving Mary through the doorway. The soldiers break the door open, swords drawn, and confront the old woman. They are looking around when the old man comes running back through the rear door.

"Where have you been?" the leader commands.

"Nowhere!" the panicked old man replies. "I haven't seen her!"

The leader groans and then orders, "Out the back door! Find her!" Without another word he thrusts the sword into the old man and runs him completely through. The old woman screams. The soldier retracts the sword and follows the others out the back door as the old man slumps to the floor. The old woman grabs him and begins to cry.

"This way, quickly," the second villager says as they hear the soldiers tromping up the small street behind the houses. The villager leads Mary and his wife out the front door and runs across the main street. By now, the noise has caused many people to open their doors. The villager, his wife and Mary all go running into the first open door. The soldiers follow them out into the main street and many doors slam closed.

"What do we do now?" asks one of the other soldiers.

"We find her," says the leader.

They begin to break in through the doors up and down the street one by one. There are screams heard and people randomly dart from their doors to escape up the street. As the soldiers return to the street in continuation of their mayhem, one points to the far end of town as he says, "Look!" They all turn to look and there are other soldiers illuminated by faint torchlight on horseback riding hard towards them.

"What do we do now?" asks one.

"We have no choice," says the leader. "Mount up!" he yells. The Roman marauders make a dash for their horses and mount up. They take off into the night and are soon followed quickly by the king's soldiers riding after them.

The sounds of horse and rider evaporates into the night air and all that is left are the wails and crying in the aftermath. Several villagers go in search of victims. Six men are dead and two women are injured, but not seriously. Two other men cling to life having been seriously wounded. Mary runs to see what happened to Sarah. She finds Sarah crying with a cut to her face. She tells Mary one of them slapped her after she refused to tell them anything.

Soon, the king's soldiers return. Esselt and Mary are there to speak to them along with a few other villagers. "We lost them. If it hadn't been so dark, we might have caught them," the rider explains. "That's probably why they came tonight. They were counting on the darkness to slip in and then escape."

"Who were they?" Esselt asks.

"They looked like Romans. That's all I could tell."

"It was a lucky thing you were here," Esselt says.

"We were passing through and just happened to camp right outside of town. One of the villagers came running and told us there were Romans killing villagers."

"It's bad," Esselt laments, "But it could've been much worse had you not been here."

"Will they come back?" Mary asks.

"Not likely," the rider says. "But I'm leaving some men at both ends of town, just in case."

"Thank you," Esselt says. "We are in your debt."

It is a long night and no one gets any sleep. Esselt and Mary are talking. "Is it over now?" Mary asks, still shaking.

"I don't know," Esselt says. "It could be, but I just don't know."

"I wish I knew why they were after me. Why now?"

"I don't know that either," Esselt laments with a large sigh.

"Sarah and I will leave in the morning."

"Why? This wasn't your doing."

"But as long as I'm here, I place the village in danger," Mary says.

"I knew of the danger and did nothing to protect the people. I'm as much to blame as anyone."

"Still… I don't want anyone facing the Romans for me."

"And why not? Are you a one woman shield? Do you never require help from anyone? Did Jesus not pick twelve disciples to help him in his ministry?" Mary nods. "We are not created to go it alone. It is this disciple support that you preach yourself, am I right?"

"Yes. You are right," Mary admits. "I just don't want to ask people to die because of me."

"If you do not allow people to be brave, how will they learn bravery? If you make them run when their faith is tested, how will their faith survive?" Esselt puts her arm around Mary, "Let us make that decision. Allow us the opportunity to help you."

Mary pats Esselt's hand on her arm, "Alright. If you insist. I trust your judgment."

"Good. The town is being watched by the soldiers. Now you and Sarah try to get some sleep."

Two days later, Mary stands outside and hears the sound of approaching horses. Her heart quickens as she looks up the street, but none of the villagers standing near the road seem panicked. As her heart pounds heavier, she calls to Sarah in the house. As Sarah comes out, a familiar coach rounds the corner of the street and makes its way to where

Mary stands. A large wave of relief flows over Mary as Sarah approaches, "What's wrong, mama?"

"I was ready to run, but everything is alright now," Mary pants as she pats her chest with her hand.

The coach rolls up and stops. A coachman cracks the door open and an unknown voice filters out. "Mary," he calls, "please, get in quickly."

"Why, what's wrong?" Mary asks as she presses close to the door.

"They are coming again. We must go to a place where you can stay. Vercingetorix wants me to take you there, but we have to go quickly. Please?"

"I'll get Sarah," Mary says.

"No!" the voice says strongly. "My instructions were just you! Get in quickly. There is no time to argue. You must trust me."

Mary turns and calls to Sarah to her. "They may be coming again," Mary says to Sarah as she grabs hold of Sarah's arms. "I am going to where the king can keep me safe. Don't worry, they will take care of you here."

"How long will you be gone?" Sarah asks panicked.

"I don't know," Mary says as she pulls Sarah to her and hugs her tightly. She then steps up onto the coach, "I'll send word to you soon. Be strong for me." Mary climbs into the coach while looking upon Sarah's worried face. Mary tries to nod one last time as if to say that everything would be fine. The coach door closes and the coachman calls out to the driver. In an instant, the coach flies away behind the sound of heavy hooves and Sarah watches Mary go as the coach is enveloped in a thin cloud of dust.

The young man to whom the voice belongs sits very quietly as the coach rocks along. The purple curtains on the windows are untied and the cloth shutters are drawn down while some light manages to squeeze through the openings around them. They rock and bounce in the dimly lit coach and the silence between them seems forced.

"How far are the Romans behind us?" Mary finally asks.

"I don't know," The young man replies.

"You said they were coming again." Mary explains.

"I'm just the messenger. I was sent to bring you to the designated place. Vercingetorix will explain everything once you get there, I'm sure." he says very mechanically. After another long silence, Mary asks, "Where are we going?"

"I don't know," the man says.

"You don't know where you're taking me?" Mary asks. Her suspicion in this whole event is becoming peaked and her voice takes on a tone of agitation. "You don't know? Or, you just won't tell me?"

"I'm not the driver," he replies calmly. "I'm a passenger – just like you."

"Why can't I see where we're going?" Mary continues.

"I was told to close the curtains so nobody could see you inside."

Once again there is a protracted silence. Whoever the young man is, he is not going to be forthcoming with lots of information. Mary decides to wait it out and settles back in the gloominess to await their destination.

"Esselt?" Sarah says excitedly as she walks up behind Esselt standing in the street speaking with two villagers. Esselt excuses herself and turns to talk to Sarah. The two of them begin to casually walk.

"Yes, child?" Esselt replies.

"A coach… it was Vercingetorix's coach… the one I've ridden in before. Vercingetorix just came in the coach and took mama away."

"Slow down, child. Vercingetorix took Mary?" Esselt asks calmly.

"Yes, in his coach. Mama said there wasn't time to explain. He was taking to her to safety."

"Did she say where?"

"No. She just said she would send word and then she left."

"Oh. Well, I suppose if it was the king, she's in as safe a place as possible. I wouldn't worry about it now."

"What should I do now?" Sarah asks confused. "I'm scared. Please tell me."

"Sarah, calm down. You have been a grown woman for some time now," Esselt explains. "You will have to find your own way eventually. A time is coming when you will have to be strong for your mother."

"That's what she told me. I don't understand."

"I know, child. Life can seem very confusing when what we need most is clarity. You can take care of yourself while she's gone, can't you?"

"Well, yes. Of course I can." Sarah quips.

"Then, do that," Esselt says.

"But, what will happen to mama?"

"I don't know," Esselt says. Then with a reassuring smile, she says, "What I *do* know is that God is watching over you both. Always follow your heart and listen for that small voice of God that lives inside you. It will always guide you in the path you need to follow. Be patient and I'm sure that your mother will return in time. Meanwhile, be strong."

"I will try," Sarah says with uncertainty. Esselt takes hold of her head and kisses her on the forehead. She then gives Sarah one last smile and turns to leave. Sarah shuffles her way back home, still not sure that she will be up to whatever is coming.

As Mary begins to nod off, the coach finally comes to a stop. The young man jumps up and opens the door to exit. Mary stirs and her body is stiff. It has been a long ride, maybe several hours, and her muscles are letting her know it. As she reaches the door, the young man waits to help her down. She grabs his hand and steps down from the coach. She stretches her back and tries to fight off a yawn, but the yawn wins and she tries to shake off her lethargy with a loud one. "Goodness," she says after finishing.

She looks around and can tell she's standing on the side of a mountain. She can see a gorgeous view of the valley below stretching out in the waning sunlight as the shadows begin to overtake the landscape. There is a small camp of Vercingetorix's guards who seem to largely ignore Mary's presence as they speak and laugh around a small fire. "Follow me," the young man beckons. Behind the guards is a small cave entrance lit by a single torch just inside the opening.

"Vercingetorix will meet with you here," the young man says as they reach a small cavern at the end of the tunnel.

"Here?" Mary exclaims. "How long do I have to wait here?"

"I do not know," the man says as he exits. "But it shouldn't be long. If you need drink, the guards will give it to you," he adds as he departs down the tunnel.

Mary begins pacing like a caged lioness. Her arms are folded as she walks next to the small fire illuminating the cavern. She then sits on a large stone next to the fire before getting up to pace again. "Wait here... Wait here, he says." She is still unsure what to think of this whole situation and begins to think that running might have been a mistake. "What will they do when they can't find me?" she mumbles to herself. She occasionally walks back down the tunnel to see if Vercingetorix has arrived. The guards always ask if she needs anything, but she is too agitated to relax. "All I want are some answers to all of this," she thinks.

Sanctuary

After waiting for what seems like a small eternity, Mary can finally hear someone coming. She stands up not knowing what to suspect. To her relief, it is Vercingetorix followed by a single guard who stops down in the tunnel before entering this space. "I am so glad to see you," Mary sighs. "I cannot wait to get out of here."

"I'm sorry," Vercingetorix replies, "but you'll have to stay here for a while longer."

"I know you want to protect me," Mary explains, "but there must be somewhere else I can hide out other than this damp cave."

"Protect you?" Vercingetorix chuckles quietly. "I want you dead."

Mary is stunned and can't believe she heard Vercingetorix correctly. "Dead?" she asked puzzled.

"If I were not surrounded by so many incompetent people, you would already be dead."

Mary slumps back down on the stone as her strength drains away. She suddenly feels disoriented and somewhat paralyzed. "I don't understand," she mumbles numbly.

"Of course you don't understand. So allow me to explain it to you," Vercingetorix says as he begins to slowly pace side to side. "I sent some of my best soldiers, who are now at the head of my list of incompetent people, to the borderlands with a simple mission. They found a small detachment of Roman soldiers and slaughtered them to get their uniforms and equipment. It was simple, but actually was no small feat due to the secrecy, I can assure you. It was also at great personal risk to my position as "Roman Liaison" to the Empire should they have been caught. It was necessary that my men looked as Roman as possible when they came to kill you so that the people would believe they were Romans."

"Those were *your* men? Those men killed villagers. Your own people," Mary says angrily.

"Somewhat regrettable - but necessary. As I said, it had to look real. But you didn't cooperate and just die, did you? No, you had to escape. But, no matter. This will work almost as well."

"If you wanted me to leave, all you had to do was tell me to go."

Vercingetorix chuckles again, "Leave? You truly do not have a clue what is going on here."

"No, I don't," Mary says confused through the beginnings of tears.

"You were *supposed* to be a martyr, Mary Magdalene! Your influence has spread throughout all of Gaul. You must understand, the clans of this land have been at war for far too long… all trying to unify the people into one clan. Then, *you* arrived. And you managed to do, almost single-handedly, what nobody else could do. Draw everyone in Gaul into one common bond. I saw the opportunity to use that. If you died at the hands of the Romans, the people would be outraged. They would finally have the resolve to unite against the Roman occupation for the love of Mary Magdalene. And they would unite under *my* banner."

"What makes you think my death would make them flock to you?" Mary asks wiping back her angry tears.

"That's where Sarah comes in," Vercingetorix says wryly.

"If you hurt her, I will kill you myself," Mary threatens.

"Hurt her? My dear, Mary… Her wellbeing is of my utmost concern. However, since you didn't die according to the plan, I can't afford the risk to kill you now as my surprise is gone. If I had just given them a dead body and claimed the Romans were responsible, it would have been much less convincing than if the people had seen it with their own eyes. But if I kill you now, they will blame me for not keeping you safe from the Romans. So, now I will inform the people that I am keeping you hidden and safe from the Romans. You will remain here for the time being, until I can decide what to do with you."

"And Sarah?"

"Yes, Sarah. I will convince her in your absence to marry my son, Litaviccos. If she still feels for him as she did before you dragged her away, I don't think it will take a large effort to convince either of them. She is now Jesus' only heir. An heir to all of the influence you have built, and as my new daughter, I will be in a position to wield her influence."

"Jesus has no blood line. Sarah is adopted," Mary argues. "The Jews among your people will not let you get away with that."

"I think they will. I will just have to see to it that this little fact will remain our little secret. And it will remain our secret if you wish her to go on living."

"Why does it matter who knows?" Mary asks.

"She is only good to me if she is a blood heir. Without that, I might as well dispose of her too. As long as the people believe that she is, she will live and this will work," Vercingetorix says arrogantly. "And when it does, all of the chieftains will be forced to concede leadership to me for fear of their people revolting because they love you more than their chieftain."

"I think you overestimate my influence over them," Mary chides.

Vercingetorix smirks, "I think you greatly underestimate it. I have no doubt most of my people would chose you over me. You have no idea how powerful you have become." Then turning aside he says, "Naturally, I will give each chieftain some power in my new kingdom. In exchange for their cooperation."

"Then you will march on the Roman Empire? You will lose," Mary says.

"Oh, I would not be so presumptuous as to think I could defeat the Roman Empire with our current forces. And, I have no intentions of jeopardizing my lucrative position as Roman Liaison. I will wage a token protest for a while using the appropriate diplomatic channels. You know, put on a good show for the people. It will not be long before they get complacent and forget all about it and we go back to where we started. Except then I will lead the kingdom, have some say over the Romans here and leave a dynasty to all my generations."

"You're delusional," Mary exclaims.

"We shall see, Mary. We shall see. In the meantime, please make yourself at home. You are a long way from anywhere and the predatory animals that inhabit this part of the world makes going for a stroll very dangerous. So, I suggest you get used to this place." Vercingetorix turns to leave and then stops. After a brief moment, he turns and says, "On second thought, feel free to take a stroll. If I bring them your mauled body, then my secret is safe and they can't blame me for letting the Romans get to you." He laughs a very hearty laugh as he exits the cave and it echoes throughout the chamber.

Vercingetorix exits the cave and says to Captain Dummacos, "You are responsible for keeping her here. Do not disappoint me again, captain."

"Yes, my lord. She will stay here until you send for her," Dummacos replies.

"Remember to feed her every now and then," Vercingetorix smiles. "I may still need her alive for something later on."

"Of course, my lord."

"And I do not want her violated," Vercingetorix snaps as a coachman opens the door to his coach. "I will kill any man who does so. I do not hold with her god, but I'm not taking any chances either." The door is closed behind him and the coach is quickly on its way back to the palace.

Mary hears someone else coming, but much quieter. Her strength has abandoned her followed closely by her hope. She doesn't try to stand when Dummacos enters the chamber carrying some supplies. "You!" Mary exclaims breathlessly as she jerks, putting her hand to her mouth. "I recognize you from the riders of that night. You were the one who came to kill me, aren't you?"

"The disadvantage of being a soldier is that you sometimes have to do what you're told," Dummacos says in an apologetic tone. "I didn't want to kill anyone that night and I get no pleasure from this duty either."

"But you did kill. You killed your own clansmen. We always have a choice. Even soldiers have a choice of who they will follow. You made yours," Mary says with disdain.

Dummacos stands speechless as Mary's words stab deeply into his guilt of that night and painfully sting his pride. Finally, he says, "I brought you some things you will need. My men and I will be outside. If there is anything

122

we are allowed to get you, we will. I'll be bringing you some food later."

"What is your name?" Mary asks.

"I am Captain Dummacos."

"Thank you for your concern, captain," Mary says coldly as she looks away. "But, I don't require anything at this time." Dummacos begins to speak, but seeing Mary in this way, thinks better of it and decides against it. He walks over to the stone where she is sitting and sets the items down. He then turns and leaves without another word. Mary can hear him shuffle down the tunnel. She then begins to mumble out loud to nobody as her head still spins with the betrayal. Half of her thoughts are a conversation with herself and the other half are directed to God. "How could he do this to me? What will I do now? What can I do now? God, I'm so sorry. What a mess I've made of this. What will happen to Sarah? Father, watch after her and keep her safe in your arms until I see her again. Will I see her again?"

Mary now stands and examines the cave in detail as she had never really noticed it, but was just waiting around to leave this place. The floor is all dirt and it is roughly square, the four walls being about thirty feet apart and twenty feet high. The ceiling is not solid and has several deep fissures. Mary cannot see any discernible light but the smoke from the small fire seems to be escaping to somewhere. To one side is the large stone on which she sat that has been hewn flat on the top to serve as both table and bed. A small fire burns in a pit dug into the dirt beside a small pile of wood that, as time goes by, the guards will periodically resupply. Several blankets are laid on the stone for Mary to sleep along with a wash basin, a water pitcher and a chamber pot for her to use.

Days pass as Mary's prison closes around her. The hours hang stale in the air as her strength languishes in a restless melancholy. She tries to sit quietly and pray, but thoughts of Sarah distract her and tears well up in her eyes until she can think of nothing else. Her captors allow her to walk to the mouth of the cave and sit for stretches of time but she does not speak to any of them. It helps her keep day separate from night and it breaks the monotony of her cave walls. By the third day, she sits to pray but now is unsure what to pray for. Her petition to God wanders from thought to thought, circling through several subjects until once more returning, as they always do, to Sarah.

On the fifth day, the guard retrieves Mary's metal plate from lunch but has left the cup of wine on the stone slab. Mary stands numb and lost in thought. She barely notices the coming and going of the guard. After the guard leaves, the cave begins to light up in a bright glow. Mary looks around confused, not knowing if the light is real or if her mind is finally going. Then Mary notices a figure standing in the cave with her. It is a female figure with long flowing hair and dressed in a long, white robe. A flower garland adorns her head. She glows with a bluish-white aura that slowly pulsates. At first, it hurts Mary's eyes to look at her and she shields her face with her hand. But once her eyes begin to adjust, she lowers her hand and stands lost for words to this unexpected visitor.

"Mary," the woman calls. Her mouth does not move and no sound escapes, but Mary hears the voice in her head.

"Is this a dream? Who are you?" Mays asks.

"I am a messenger sent from Jesus... sent from God," Mary hears in her head. Mary feels her strength drain away and her legs become weak. She stumbles and begins to fall, but the woman catches her and leads Mary to sit on the stone.

"Why are you here? What is the message?" Mary struggles to say.

"Do not be troubled, Mary." The woman reaches out her hand once more and caresses Mary's face. With her touch, Mary can feel her strength return. There is a calm that overcomes her.

"You are an angel… from heaven."

"Yes," Mary hears in her head as the woman smiles. "Do not be afraid. I come to comfort you in this hour of darkness. You, among others, are still highly favored by God."

"Why will he not rescue me?"

"The hand of God moves among the world of men. It is not for men, nor angels, to say by what path it will take."

"I don't understand," Mary says confused.

"You were not supposed to come, but you did."

"I know. Forgive me, please," Mary pleads.

"There is no sin in you that has not already been forgiven. But there are things of this world that, once in motion, cannot be stopped for one person. Or, at least, will not be stopped."

"I see," Mary sighs. "I must remain here because of what I have put into motion."

"This curse is yours alone, Mary Magdalene. You will never leave this cave until you are called home."

"Then call me home now. Please," Mary pleads again.

"That is not within my power to answer, Mary. For now, you must remain. I do not know why."

"What about Sarah?" Mary asks. "What will happen to her?"

"It is unclear. She will be pulled in many directions. What she will do is hers to decide."

"Is there nothing I can do to help her?"

"What all you could do, you have already done. You have taught her all that is necessary to help her. You have been a good friend and a good teacher to her. She will never forget your teachings for as long as she lives in this world."

"So I have to just sit here?" Mary asks in a depressed voice.

"Patience, Mary. God has not left you. Here," Mary hears as the woman waves her hand over the slab. "This is manna; like God gave to Moses." As Mary hears this, small, white pieces of a fluffy substance appear on the slab. "Take and eat." It looks like meat but is light in weight like fine bread. Mary takes a piece and puts it into her mouth. As she chews, she waits to taste something. It really has no flavor at all, but leaves her with a whisper of a sweet sensation somehow. When she swallows it and picks up another, she begins to feel better. When she swallows the second piece, her melancholy seems to fade away. Her spirit improves and her mind settles. By the time she finishes what sets on the slab, she feels refreshed and focused.

"Much better," Mary hears. "I will return to you, so do not despair."

"Wait…" Mary pleads but the woman and the light disappear leaving her as she was before, but feeling much better about it. For the first time in a long time, she is able to sit unfettered and pray.

THE SACRIFICE

"I'm worried about her, Vio" Sarah says through her tears. "She should've been back by now." She and Litaviccos sit on a bench in the courtyard of the palace. Litaviccos holds Sarah in his arms and tries to comfort her, but Sarah is inconsolable. As they sit, Vercingetorix enters the courtyard.

Litaviccos stands, "Father, where is Mary?" Sarah holds back her tears and waits for an answer as she looks to Vercingetorix. There is a silence as Vercingetorix studies both their faces.

"Will you excuse us, Litaviccos?" Vercingetorix asks. "I would have a word with Sarah is private."

After some hesitation, Litaviccos replies dutifully, "Of course, Father. I will return to my duties until you need me." He grabs Sarah's hand between both of his and says softly, "We'll see each other later." Sarah nods and Litaviccos exits quickly.

In an apprehensive tone, Sarah turns back to Vercingetorix and asks, "Tell me. What has happened to my mother?"

Vercingetorix makes his way to the bench and sits on the other end from Sarah. "Your mother is fine, dear. You should not be upset for her."

"Where is she? What has happened?"

"Well... It seems that things have gotten complicated," Vercingetorix begins to explain.

"Complicated?"

"What do you know of your mother's relationship with this man Jesus?" Vercingetorix asks wryly.

"She loved him very much, I know that. She and Jesus were very close."

"She was wise not to tell you everything." Vercingetorix muses.

"Everything? What is going on? Where is she?"

"As I said, you don't have to worry about her at the moment. I have her in hiding for now. But, I don't know how long she will have to stay there."

"Hiding from what?"

"Oh, you poor child," Vercingetorix says in the most sympathetic voice he can conjure. "Your mother told me everything. Let me start at the beginning..." He stands up and folds his arms. He paces back and forth in front of the bench, only glancing to Sarah occasionally. "It turns out that Mary was married to this man Jesus. She was his wife. There were some Jews that wanted his power and they betrayed him. They struck a secret alliance with the Romans and together they conspired to kill him. You've heard of the persecutions?"

"Well, yes..." Sarah says confused. "It's because Rome sees Jesus as a threat because they think he claims an earthly kingdom."

"That's what your mother told you and it's partly true. The rest of the truth is that they are searching for those who hold Jesus's power. As his wife, they are searching for Mary. And, they will not rest until they've killed her."

"His wife? She never told me that. But, she never said she wasn't either."

"She was trying to protect you. She didn't want you to be worried that you too are being hunted."

"Me?" Sarah exclaims.

"You are his daughter. You are the only heir to Jesus' legacy."

"I'm not his daughter. Mary is not my real mother," Sarah says panicked.

"Mary has taken you as a daughter. By the law, you are as much Jesus's daughter as if you were born of his seed. You too are now the hunted."

"What am I going to do?" Sarah pleads.

"Calm down, child. I can protect you and your mother, as long as you never tell *anyone* this secret. Not even my son. You are safe as long as you remain here and no one knows that Mary was married to Jesus and you are his daughter. You must tell no one, not even Litaviccos."

"You're going to hide me with my mother?"

"Your face is not known to the Romans. You can stay safely here. But your mother has chosen to remain out of sight. She told me to tell you not to worry. She is doing this to protect you, Sarah. She wants no evil to come to you."

"Where is she?"

"I cannot tell you. She told me not to disclose where she is to anyone, not even you. If Rome found out that you knew where she was, they would double their efforts to hunt you down. And I cannot always tell who I can trust with this powerful a secret. The fewer people who know where she is hiding, the safer she is from the Romans. You *do* want your mother safe? Don't you?"

"Yes, of course," Sarah says dejectedly. "What can I do to help her?"

"I can't think of anything," Vercingetorix says as he shakes his head. "If your mother were here, she could rally the strength of those who follow this Jesus now. It would probably be half of the entire region of Gaul. Wait,"

Vercingetorix's voice trails off as if he suddenly has a thought. "Maybe you could do that."

"Do what?" ask Sarah

"You could rally the followers of Jesus to stand against the Romans on behalf of your mother. If they stood united, Rome would consider it too large a risk to come and find her."

"I don't know how to do that," Sarah laments.

"Oh, of course you don't." Vercingetorix quips. "What was I thinking? I could, *of course*, do something like that. But I forget... you are not me, are you?"

"You could? You could rally them for me? Could you do it, please? To save my mother?" Sarah pleads.

"Oh, well... you know that normally I would do anything for you and your mother, but..."

"What's wrong? Why can't you do it?"

"If I were to help you build an army, the other chieftains would see it as a political move and then they would be upset with both of us. It could lead to more war. Now, if you were *my* daughter instead of Mary's, then I could do it with no problems."

"Oh, I see," Sarah laments again.

"Well, there might be a way..." Vercingetorix says as he rubs his chin with his hand.

"What?" Sarah chirps.

"Well, it just now occurred to me... If you were to marry Litaviccos, you would be both my daughter and Mary's. Mary and I would then be related and I could combine our armies to stand and protect your mother." Vercingetorix proclaims.

"Marry Vio?"

"Does that prospect disturb you?"

"No. I mean... I was already thinking about it, but..." Sarah says lost in thought.

"It's the only way to save your mother," Vercingetorix whispers. "Would you not sacrifice that in order to help her?"

Sarah swallows deeply, "It's not really a sacrifice. And it will protect mama…"

"It's your only option to save your mother," he whispers again.

"Does Vio want to marry me?" Sarah muses.

"He does, I know it."

"Ok," Sarah says with a deep sigh, "I will marry Vio."

A deep smile grows from Vercingetorix's lips. "Excellent. Why don't you go to your room and have a nap. You look tired. I'll talk to Litaviccos."

"Yes, that sounds like a good idea. I am a little tired." Sarah walks to the edge of the courtyard and then stops when Vercingetorix calls her name. She looks over her shoulder.

"Remember, let's keep this secret of you and your mother just between us; your life and your mother's depends on it," Vercingetorix nods. "Don't worry. It'll be fine."

Litaviccos enters the chamber room through the door, "You wanted to see me, father?"

Vercingetorix is seated at a desk and writing a document. "Come in son." Litaviccos stops in front of the desk. Vercingetorix says without looking up from the desk, "You are the prince of this tribe. And now I call upon you. Are you ready to do your service to me and your people?"

"I am ready!" Litaviccos says with pride as he straightens and stands a little taller. "What must I do?"

Vercingetorix stands and looks him in the eye, "I want you to marry Sarah."

Litaviccos's stiffness disappears and his breath escapes, "What?"

Vercingetorix drops the quill and walks around the desk. "I want you marry Sarah. It is so unpleasant a task?"

"No," Litaviccos says flustered. "No. Not at all. But I don't understand."

"You don't have to understand it all right now. But it is important that Mary Magdalene and I be united against our common foes. It will allow us to protect both Mary and Sarah. Your marriage to Sarah will seal the security of our land for many generations to come."

"I love her. But will she marry me?"

"I already know that she will. So, do you accept this responsibility?"

"With pleasure," Litaviccos smiles. "If only all the tasks you ask of me were this pleasant." Vercingetorix laughs and slaps Litaviccos on the shoulder.

"Well then, perhaps you should go to her and start making plans," Vercingetorix suggests.

"I will. Thank you, father."

A knock comes at Sarah's door. "Enter," Sarah calls. Litaviccos busts in and stands by the door. "Prince Litaviccos," Sarah utters in surprise.

Litaviccos laughs, "How long has been since you've addressed me like that?" Sarah's eyes dart to the maid servant standing in the room. "Oh," he says with embarrassment.

Sarah says teasingly, "It is not proper for a prince to appear in a maiden's room unannounced." The servant girl covers her mouth to stifle her giggle.

"Oh... Um... Of course," Litaviccos says growing deeper in his embarrassment. "But I have something to ask you."

"And I you. Go to the courtyard and I will come to you there shortly," Sarah says shooing him out of the room.

"Of course, as you wish," Litaviccos says beating a hasty exit.

Sarah and the servant girl both giggle once the door is closed. "You hold the heart of the prince in your hands," the girl says.

"I know," Sarah beams. "He waits to ask me to marry him"

"Are you sure?"

"If he does not, then I will ask him," Sara says confidently.

"My lady!" the girl says shocked. There is a silence as they look at each other and then they both giggle again.

"I want to change my clothes if I am to be proposed to. Help me, please?" Sara coos breathlessly. The girl nods her head.

Wedding Bells

Litaviccos sits nervously on the bench in their favorite courtyard. The birds are singing in the trees and the trickling of water can be heard in the small fountain. He is happy as his thoughts wander and he imagines having Sarah for his wife.

Despite living in the palace, Sarah has always dressed as a girl of meager means. But she comes to the courtyard in a blue dress she has been saving for a special occasion. As Litaviccos looks up to see her, Sarah's face is beaming in anticipation of something which she has long desired. As Litaviccos rises to greet her, he stops and seems frozen in place. Sarah's smile fades, "What's wrong, Vio?"

"Oh, nothing," Litaviccos stammers. "I've never seen you look so beautiful."

Sarah can feel her face blush as she touches her check with her hand. She walks to Litaviccos and they sit on the bench. "Do you really think so?" Sarah asks.

"Yes. You are the most beautiful woman in the entire kingdom."

"I think the sun has blinded you," Sarah says with a smile.

"Then may I always be blinded by your beauty."

"Vio? You've never talked to me like this before."

"I've never had the courage to ask you to marry me before."

"Courage?" Sarah asks puzzled.

134

"I know your mother wants you to marry a Jew. I didn't think she would approve of you marrying me."

"She probably still doesn't." Sarah laments. "But with her in hiding, I have to decide for myself. She always told me to follow my heart. And my heart tells me this is the right thing to do."

"So, you would marry me over her objection... out of obligation to save your mother?"

"Yes... and no. I have loved you for a long time..."

"You have?" Litaviccos interrupts.

Sarah giggles, "Yes. I will marry you for love first and obligation second." There is a silence and Sarah says teasingly, "That is, if you get around to asking. Are you?"

Litaviccos blushes slightly, "Sorry. Yes! I am asking you to marry me and be my wife."

Sarah caresses his cheek with her hand, "I accept." She draws near to him and they kiss. It is a long kiss after which Sarah says, "When?"

"When what?" Litaviccos says lost in the moment.

Sarah smirks, "When will we get married, silly?"

"Oh," Litaviccos nods his head, "yes... when? When would you like to have the ceremony?"

"Tomorrow?" Sarah coos.

"Tomorrow?" Litaviccos laughs. "Oh no, no, no. That's impossible. It must be a big event. It will take a least a month to organize."

"Does it have to be?" Sarah wrinkles her brow.

"You must understand," Litaviccos explains, "you are marrying into the king's family. You're not just marrying me, you will be Princess Sarah. Maybe someday even Queen Sarah. Your obligation will not be to just your mother, it will be to every person in our land."

"I hadn't thought of it that way," Sarah say soberly.

"It is a burden of responsibility that we both must bear." There is another silence. Litaviccos places his hand on Sarah's face and she turns to look into his eyes. "Still want to marry me now?" Litaviccos says playfully.

Sarah throws herself into his arms and they embrace, "No matter what comes, I will marry you."

"No matter what comes," Litaviccos whispers.

Litaviccos walks into the room where Sarah and one of her servants, Enid, sit looking at material. Enid is close to Sarah's age and has become more than a servant to Sarah. She is becoming her friend and confidant in Mary's absence.

"I can't decide," Enid says.

Sarah calls to Litaviccos who stops and spins around, "Vio, what do you think? Green or yellow?"

"What?" Litaviccos asks confused. "I don't understand the question."

"Do you think I'd look better in this green?" Sarah asks as she holds up the material. "Or do you like this yellow better?"

"I don't know," says Litaviccos. "You would look lovely in either one, my sweet."

"Men! You'll make some king," Sarah says annoyed. "Can you not choose between two colors?"

"Oh very well," Litaviccos says impatiently. "Green!"

"Did you talk to your father?" Sarah asks as she holds the green material back up.

"Not yet," Litaviccos says sheepishly.

"I want mama here for the wedding, Vio" Sarah says with disdain.

"Yes, yes. I'll speak to him," Litaviccos says. He then exits the room quickly before she can entrap him in another question. After he exits the room Sarah looks at Enid with a pout.

"But I think I like the yellow better," Sarah mumbles. She then grins a bit and says, "I think we'll do yellow." Enid giggles.

The two begin to discuss some more when a knock come to the door. "Enter!" Sarah commands. A messenger appears in the open doorway carrying a small wood box. "My lady?" he calls to Sarah. Sarah looks around to see him and immediately drops everything and jumps to her feet.

"You found it?" Sarah squeaks as she rushes to meet him.

"This is the only box that matched your description."

Sarah takes the container from him and says, "Thank you very much. That will be all." The man excuses himself and closes the door behind him.

"What is that?" Enid asks. Sarah walks over and places the box on the table. She slowly removes the lid and beholds the wedding veil setting inside. She retrieves the veil and gently places it on her head.

"Where did you get that?" Enid says barely above a whisper.

"Mama made it for me," Sarah says reverently. She fluffs it around her face before removing it and lovingly placing it back in the box.

"But it's blue..." Enid says.

"So?" Sarah replies.

"It doesn't match the green or the yellow," Enid explains.

"It doesn't matter," Sarah says teary eyed. "Mama will be with me one way or the other." Sarah gently strokes the material.

"I know how much you want her to be here," Enid tries to console her. "It should be her helping you prepare for this instead of me."

Sarah turns and reaches for Enid's hand to hold, "But I'm glad you're here since she can't be. Thank you."

"You're welcome, my lady," Enid blushes.

"How many times have I asked you not to call me that?" Sarah bemoans. "You are my friend, not merely a servant. My mother taught me that I'm no better than you."

"It is so strange to hear you say that," Enid confesses.

"Why?"

"All my life I've trained to work in the palace. It is a great honor. To work here is so much better than living... out there," Enid says searching for words. "We were told over and over how we were lucky and not to forget how unworthy we were compared to those of noble birth."

"I don't believe that," Sarah interrupts.

"Then fate brings me here to serve you and have you treat me so kind," Enid says as she also becomes teary eyed.

Sarah hugs her. "Stop it," Sarah commands. "In God's eyes were are all to be servants. Jesus said whoever would be honored in his kingdom must be willing to serve everyone; the rich and the poor." There is a protracted silence and then Sarah says, "Come on, help me cut out some of this yellow material."

It is two months before the wedding day finally arrives. The preparations are enormous. The announcement is made and Vercingetorix sends messengers throughout all of Gaul spreading the news to the followers of Jesus, not only of the wedding, but also that Mary had been attacked by the Romans and is in hiding. The king spares no expense to bring the ceremony to fruition. In order to draw the followers of the Christ into the wedding and strengthen

Sarah's link with them, the ceremony will combine elements of both local and Jewish traditions.

"There you are," Litaviccos sighs. Sarah is sitting on the bench in the garden crying on the eve of the wedding. "I'm sorry."

Sarah looks at him from behind red, puffy cheeks, "It's not fair. He won't let mama even come to the wedding."

"He said it was your mother's choice," Litaviccos tries to explain. "It would make her an easy target. He says he can't truly protect her until after we're married."

"No," Sarah sobs. "She would find a way to be here. Your father is not letting her come."

"Sarah, I love you more than life. But I can't call my father a liar. Even if it were true."

"So you think it was her decision too?"

"Yes… I think so… She is trying to protect you the only way she knows how." Litaviccos draws her into his arms. "The wedding is tomorrow and then my father will be able to do something about this. This nightmare will end soon. I promise you will see your mother again as soon as it is possible." He looks into her eyes as he cradles her face. He wipes a tear away with his thumb and kisses her gently. "Please, we will carry her in our hearts." Sarah nods and then falls back into his arms.

"I'm scared, Vio," Sarah sobs. "I'm sorry but I don't know why. Maybe it's mama. Maybe it's just because this is the biggest step I've ever taken. I would just feel better if she were here."

"You don't have to marry me if you're not ready," Litaviccos says soberly.

Sarah pulls back to look him in the eyes. "Oh, no Vio," Sarah says apologetically. "I've never wanted anything more in my life." She caresses the side of his face and manages a grin. "Enid told me I'd be nervous right before. She said she was petrified the night before she got married. I'll be fine tomorrow." She falls back into the security of his arms and he holds her tightly in the silence.

The day of the wedding begins in picturesque fashion. A beautiful sunrise into a cloudless sky. Sarah is nervous as a host of servants flit around her like hummingbirds preparing the bride-to-be. Enid keeps saying how beautiful she looks while directing all the activity. Litaviccos is anxious for it all to be over with as he sits and waits while his mother picks and fusses over him. Vercingetorix takes a last walk through the area getting reports from this person and that person that all preparations are in place. A large crowd is gathered and more are arriving. The kingdom is emptying for miles in every direction.

The venue prepared is a large flat area on top of a hill outside the palace walls. There is a large circle of colored cobble stones laid out in a pattern that resembles a large comet with a swirling, spiral tail. There are spots where some of the stones are missing or are broken as time and age have misplaced the luster of the original image. It is ringed with standing stones about five feet apart. Each stone is a roughly hewn cube and stands a little more than one foot tall. Some of the stones are missing, but most of the pattern is complete. There is a stone obelisk which stands about four foot high in the center of the circle. It also shows the marks and chips of age and neglect. It's meaning and significance is of an ancient time and is lost on those that gather here today. Litaviccos choses it because it somehow feels more special than the palace and it is a favorite landmark to the inhabitants, even if they do not have a clue as to its significance. This is not the first wedding to be held here, nor will it be the last. The crowd presses to the circle as everyone jockeys for a place to see and the whole area becomes a large sea of people with just the circle as its island. The crowd begins to part to allow Litaviccos to pass through. It quickly flows back together behind him like water in his wake. Litaviccos enters the circle and he sees two of the disciples who were trained by Mary dressed all in green. They will perform the marriage. Litaviccos is in golden pants and shirt. His thin, short crown and other royal regalia make him a dashing young figure as the people give him a polite bow when he passes. Only his bare feet, an old local tradition, seem out of place. He walks to the center of the circle where the disciples also give a polite bow.

There are musicians off to one side of the circle and they begin to play harps and lutes. The crowd parts once more and Sarah walks to the edge of the circle. She is wearing a rather revealing yellow dress in comparison to her normal attire. It was made especially for this day by the King's tailor and has a definite Celtic look to it. Her hair is wrapped on top of her head in the shape of a conch shell and is contained under the light blue veil covering her head and face. She carries a bouquet of wildflowers and Enid follows behind her also carrying wildflowers. Sarah walks tenderly over the cobblestones with her bare feet as she approaches the center. As she nears Litaviccos, she reaches out and takes his extended hand and comes along beside him. One of the disciples opens with prayer and the ceremony ends twenty minutes later when they are hand-fasted together. After that, Sarah kneels before the king and removes her veil. He places a small, petite crown upon her head. Litaviccos and Sarah then embrace and kiss after being joined together to the cheers of the crowd and several cries of, "Long live Princess Sarah!"

There is a great feast in the palace and it is Sarah's idea that the generous scraps be taken outside to be passed out to the poor. After thanking their guest and saying goodbye several times, trying their best to escape, the two of them finally find themselves alone, walking to the prince's room. Arm in arm they approach the door and Litaviccos reaches out and swings it open. They enter the room and the door is closed as they stand looking into each other's eyes by the dim light cast by two small candles nearby.

"I can't believe we're finally here," Sarah whispers.

"I know. It *has* been a long day, hasn't it?" Litaviccos sighs.

"It will take me a long time to get used to being 'Princess' Sarah," she says as she stares at the crown before setting it on the table.

"And someday, queen."

"I can't even imagine that," Sarah says as she turns back towards Litaviccos. There is another silence as they stand staring at each other. After removing his crown and setting it next to Sarah's, Litaviccos reaches up and begins to unwrap Sarah's hair with a tender hand as it falls back to her shoulders. She begins to remove her dress and Litaviccos reaches out to snuff the candles. Litaviccos lays her in the bed and Sarah closes her eyes and is lost in the moment as Litaviccos runs his hand over her creamy skin. At last, her most inner desire has finally come to fruition. They flow together as the moonlight pours through the large window and the marriage is consummated.

Hail The New King

Only a week passes before Vercingetorix feels ready to begin flexing his newly found influence muscle. He sends word to all the clans that they must come to his palace and meet for a matter of great and urgent importance. There are many who balk at coming and threaten to decline Vercingetorix's invitation. But one by one, Vercingetorix convinces them all to come. It is a gathering that has not happened in an age, since Vercingetorix's father was a lad. To have all the clans represented in one room was an historic event and many watched to see what would unfold. That day had finally come.

Several chieftains sit around a square table. Servants stand at the ready to fill tankards with ale as they drink and argue. They sit with nervous anticipation and each sharp noise and motion creates a jump or fidget. There is a fragile, uneasy peace that hangs in the room, ready to break at the slightest indiscretion. Silence overcomes the room as the door swings open and a large, scraggly warrior tromps in behind a servant that turns and motions him into the room. He stops and stares at the seated warriors sitting at the table. One of the warriors slams his hand on the table as he stands and the two exchange piercing stares. "Ambiorix!" the chieftain that stands up says. There is an awkward silence. "I thought I already killed you last year," The chieftain says with only a hint of sarcasm.

Ambiorix finally begins to walk to an empty chair, "Only in your dreams, Catuvolcos…" He lays a large, engraved greatsword on the table and sits in the chair.

Catuvolcos points his outstretched finger at Ambiorix, "Next time, I will. You can…" He is interrupted as Vercingetorix comes busting into the room with a giant smile and outstretched arms.

"Welcome my brother chieftains," Vercingetorix says boisterously.

"Why are we here, Vercingetorix?" Catuvolcos demands still standing.

"Please, sit. Sit down and relax," Vercingetorix chides. Catuvolcos sits slowly as Vercingetorix circles the room.

"Your manhood indeed hangs low for you to call a meeting of this council," Ambiorix states. "Especially when every man here would like to see you split open and your entrails scattered across the kingdom, as you have cheated each one of us." The comment draws a laugh from most of those present.

"Such venom hardly becomes you, Ambiorix," Vercingetorix scoffs. "Can we not talk for one day as brothers?"

"Give back the lands your father has stolen from me and I will greet you as brother," Ambiorix howls.

"The lands your father has stolen from all of us," Catuvolcos adds.

"Brothers, what causes me to call this council," Vercingetorix boasts ignoring both of them, "is that we have come to the day that peace comes to Gaul." This also draws a laugh from the majority assembled.

"And who is to lead this new peaceful Gaul? You?" Catuvolcos laughs.

"Yes," Vercingetorix says calmly.

"You have been at your own mead if you think we will follow you," says another.

"Why would we follow you? Please, entertain us with your tale," Catuvolcos teases.

"You have, no doubt, come to know Mary Magdalene?" Vercingetorix asks.

"She is a scourge," Ambiorix says in disgust. "Her people spread through my kingdom like the dye the women used to color the cloth. They touch everything and the peasants turn to her teachings and dedicate their souls to her god." He spits on the floor.

"She saved my son," Bituitus responds. "Without her, I would have no heir. I am too feeble to sire another son."

"She healed a sickness that was spreading through my clan and would have left me a chieftain to no one," says another.

"She is still dangerous," Ambiorix responds.

"Not anymore," Vercingetorix says slyly.

"Stop threshing the wind Vercingetorix, and get to the point. What does this Mary have to do with us? And why have you summoned us?" Catuvolcos demands.

"Mary is in hiding from the Jews and Romans who are trying to kill her," Vercingetorix begins. "The reason she is hunted, as I have discovered, is that she is the wife of Jesus, King of all Jews."

"His wife?" Catuvolcos asks.

"Yes," Vercingetorix continues. "Sarah, who is her daughter and the only blood-line heir of Jesus' kingship and Mary's influence, has married my son, Litaviccos." Many of the chieftains stand up outraged and an argument begins to ensue. "Please! Please, my brothers. Sit! There is no need for fighting." Order returns to the room and the chieftains sit once again. Looks of mistrust and skepticism cover their faces. "As I was saying, Princess Sarah is now my daughter. There's nothing you can do now to change that. So, by marriage, I now claim the right to Mary's people on behalf of that daughter."

"We will not sit by while you do this," Catuvolcos demands.

"You begin a war like no other," Ambiorix yells.

"No," Vercingetorix says calmly with a smile, "You've already told us that most of your kingdom would flock to Mary's banner before your own, Ambiorix. Are you ready for rebellion among your own kingdom if you chose to stand against Sarah and Mary?" The room grows deathly silent. "If you force me to draw all those sympathetic to Mary to myself, I will empty your kingdoms and then whom will you war with?"

"It won't happen like that," Ambiorix says.

"Are you willing to find out? Vercingetorix asks.

"What are you proposing?" Bituitus softly asks knowing that he has already pledged everything to this God of Mary.

"Simple," Vercingetorix explains. "Each of you will support me as Supreme Chieftain over all clans in Gaul. In exchange, I will make you Governing Chieftain over the clans you already rule. Then, in a time of peace, we can build a real army right under the nose of the Romans. We will grow wealthy because we're not paying for the privilege of killing each other. The people will make us prosperous."

"The Romans will not allow that," Ambiorix says.

"I am the eyes and ears of Rome here. They will only learn what I tell them. We have been warring among ourselves for so long, they have learned to ignore us. I say, let them ignore us. We will grow strong while they look the other way. Then, one day, we will be strong enough to rid ourselves of this Roman plague. For that is the *real* plague here." There is another deathly silence and their looks of mistrusts are beginning to turn to looks of contemplation.

"Think well on it, my brothers. I will expect your answer in the morning." The door swings open and Vercingetorix slips out of the room leaving the chieftains exchanging glances.

The next morning, Vercingetorix sits at the desk writing a scroll in his study. The door opens and a servant waves Ambiorix into the room. Vercingetorix barely gives Ambiorix a glance as he walks up to the desk. "Have you come to a decision?" Vercingetorix asks.

"Well, well," Ambiorix muses. "It seems you finally have gained an upper hand. It seems we don't have much of a choice."

"You speak for the council then?"

"I do. We have decided that maybe it is time to give something else a chance. So, we would basically keep what we have?"

"Of course. I only want the opportunity to bring peace to all our people."

"Don't play games with me, Vercingetorix. I know you too well. You are power hungry and you don't give a second thought about your people." Vercingetorix looks away and a grin breaks onto his face. "We will give you your wish… for now. But I warn you, if you try to cheat us the way your father cheated our fathers, it will be all out war and it will be you against the entire council."

Vercingetorix retrieves a piece of parchment from the desk and places it in front of Ambiorix, "Just have all the Governing Chieftains sign this with their marks."

Ambiorix looks at Vercingetorix with a look of disbelief as he reaches for the small parchment. He begins to read it and mumbles, "You dirty mule! We don't even get a say in this? You've already written it all up."

"As you've said, you've run out of choices. Besides, it is exactly what we discussed. Nothing more, nothing less. Just sign it and you're on your way to becoming richer than you are now."

Within the day, Vercingetorix receives the parchment back. Each chieftain has made his mark and imprinted his seal next to it. Vercingetorix calls for a festival to be held two days later. Many of the outlaying population come to the palace to hear the news and take in the festival. There are great spectacles and all forms of performances and magic illusions and singing and dancing and plenty of drinking.

Early one afternoon, Vercingetorix speaks on the palace green from a specially constructed platform to as many people who can cram into the space. He is in his full regalia, as are all the chieftains, and is surrounded by them on the platform, Ambiorix to his right and Catuvolcos to his left. Litaviccos and Sarah are also there but are far more casually dressed and stand well off to one side. Vercingetorix throws up his hands to quiet the crowd. "Today is an historic day," Vercingetorix begins to shout. "Today all my people… all *our* people," Vercingetorix corrects himself as he places his hands on the shoulder of Ambiorix and Catuvolcos, "finally enter into a time of lasting peace between the clans." A cheer rises from the crowd. "The chieftains of every tribe band together today in an accord which will put an end to the war between us." Another cheer. "Let us put aside our past disputes and embrace everyone from all clans as our brothers. As leader, I appoint each of my fellow chieftains as governor over all the undisputed lands they currently possess. Of the disputed territories, those will be divided equitably and fairly in time. But today is a day to raise a cup and celebrate as a united people."

Vercingetorix turns away with a raised hand to the cheers and chants of the crowd. "You see?" Vercingetorix says to the chieftains assembled. "The people are ready for peace. Stick to this accord and you will receive everything you've desired, and more." They leave the platform and return to the castle. Litaviccos and Sarah linger behind and nonchalantly make their way into the center of town.

The people are dancing and reveling in the city square as the announcement sifts its way through the crowd like ink soaking into paper. The new princess drags the prince along to mingle with the common people gathered and they blend in almost unnoticeably. There are women who hug Sarah as they pass by and men who firmly pat the prince on his back and shoulders. They sample some of the food and both join in the dancing. They are soon exhausted and find themselves at a table with a cup of ale.

"You're amazing," Litaviccos says trying to catch his breath.

"Why do you say that?" Sarah replies also catching her breath. "I don't dance that well."

"No, not that," Litaviccos replies. "It's just the way you seem to relate with these people."

"I don't understand," Sarah says confused. "You mean because they're poor?"

"That. But even more than that. You're a foreigner and still you seem to fit in where ever you go or whoever you're with."

Sarah sips her ale, "That's because I just think of them as people, I guess."

"Now I don't understand," Litaviccos says sipping his ale. "They're subjects and you and I are royalty."

"I wasn't always a princess, silly," Sarah says. "We are all the same." From the look on Litaviccos's face, Sarah

149

can see that he isn't convinced. "God made us all," Sarah continues. "Being prince or king, just means you're the leader. But look around you. Everyone you see is a father or a mother or a son or a daughter just like you and me. Each of them wants to live a happy life… to feed their children… to know love. All of them have problems – maybe not as big as yours – but their problems tug at them just as much as yours do. All of them want the same things you and I want; for their lives to mean something. So, you treat them like you would treat yourself. Treat them like you would want to be treated if things were reversed."

"I never thought about them like that," Litaviccos whispers in contemplation.

"Mama taught me that," Sarah whispers back. She begins to fight back the tears as Litaviccos asks, "What's wrong?"

"Oh, nothing," Sarah says as she wipes at her eyes. "I just wish mama was here to see this. I miss her."

"I know," Litaviccos replies.

"Now that there is peace, surely mama can come back to us and be well protected here," Sarah reasons.

"It makes sense to me," Litaviccos says.

Sarah slaps her cup down on the table, "Then talk to your father and make him understand that mama needs to come home."

Litaviccos shifts uncomfortably and then says hesitantly, "Ok, I will."

"Vio!..." Sarah says with urgency.

"I will!" Litaviccos says firmly.

The Vision

Mary's life becomes a string of melancholy days in which she wanders in and out of dreams and thoughts and boredom. Dummacos usually brings Mary her food and only misses coming when he's been called away. Dummacos always tries to make some small talk but Mary shuns his attempts. This is the man that tried to kill her and she will have none of his company. As this relationship matures however, she becomes convinced that Dummacos is the most polite of all of the guards who wait on her.

His persistent preoccupation with speaking to her wears her down and she finds herself unwittingly engaging in polite conversations. Mary begins to complain to Dummacos about the conditions she is having to endure. That prompts Dummacos to have a bed and a chair brought into to the cave for Mary, along with extra blankets and wash towels. He surprises her one day by bringing her lunch on fine plates instead of the tin platter she usually gets. Mary's heart begins to soften over time and she begins to have genuine conversations with Dummacos as he keeps her informed of Sarah's life and news from the outside. She is careful to never get too personal as she refuses to open herself up to that.

One morning, she is greeted by Dummacos as he brings in breakfast. He has just returned from a week of being absent in the camp. This morning, there are pastries included.

With a sarcastic smile, Mary asks, "Pastries? Where did you get these? Or did you make them yourself?"

"No," Dummacos chuckles. "I arrived back here this morning. Those come from the palace."

"Really? Is Vercingetorix that concerned about my diet now?" Mary inquires teasingly.

"Vercingetorix doesn't know."

"What?" Mary acts astonished. "You did this yourself?"

"Yes," Dummacos smiles and nods his head. "All of it. The food, the bed, the chair... I had all of it brought here."

"Really?" Mary now asks in a more serious tone. "I thought you cleared all this through Vercingetorix."

Dummacos turns away. "No," he shakes his head. "He told me I was to keep you here and to keep you alive. But he failed to specify in what manner that was to be accomplished. He would have you live like a dog. But he doesn't see you every day... see your sadness. I am not like him. I couldn't bear that."

"So I have you to thank for all of this?" Mary whispers. Dummacos nods his head. Mary snaps out of her emotion and says more coldly, "Well, thank you captain. I shall remember you more kindly in my prayers." There is an awkward silence before Dummacos says, "My lady," and retreats from the cave.

In her meditation that evening, she does think kindly of Dummacos in the beginning. "Perhaps I'm wrong about him," Mary thinks. "He's only doing his job. But he's not just doing his job; he seems to actually care about people other than himself. He's funny and kind... And he does keep me informed about Sarah; which I forgot to ask him about before I chased him off. That's the only thing that brings me comfort here. Now I'm thinking that the news is all him as well. Wait! What am I thinking? This is still the man that tried to kill me. And will probably kill me still.

He's just a soldier after all, isn't he? I know he's going to have to kill me eventually. He's kind to me so I'll cooperate and won't try to escape. Perhaps I can make him my ally. Perhaps I can trick him into helping me escape this place with Sarah. It's worth a try. Then when Vercingetorix finds out that he helped us escape, Vercingetorix will have him killed for sure. Perhaps that will be the instrument of our revenge. It's probably not any more than he deserves. But, can I be that evil? Will I hate myself if I do this? No, I'm doing this for Sarah. It has to be done!"

It is a beautiful day as the sun climbs into a bright sky. Dummacos brings her breakfast and has returned to his men. It's time to see if the plan will work. Mary walks down the dimly lit tunnel to the outside and sits just inside the opening to let the sun shine on her face. Captain Dummacos sees her and walks over with a stool and sits with his back to the wall just outside the opening so that there is no direct line of sight between them so it will not look too suspicious. "Do you require anything, my lady?" Dummacos asks.

"Stop calling me that," Mary sighs. "It makes me sound like I'm somehow important. Just call me Mary."

"As you wish… Mary. Do you need me to bring you anything?"

"What I need, you cannot bring me," Mary says despondently.

"What do you desire?"

"My daughter," Mary snaps. "Bring me my daughter that I might speak to her one more time." Dummacos has no response. "I'm sorry," Mary sighs. "It's not all your fault. How is she?"

"The same. Still worried. Still like a swarming fly in Vercingetorix's ear. She will never give up on you, my la... sorry, Mary"

"She is my strength and my blessing, now. All that I have left," Mary sighs. "I cannot bear the thought of her being the daughter of Vercingetorix. Or living under his influence."

"She is too much like her mother," Dummacos chuckles. "She neither asks for nor heads any of his council." Mary also chuckles. "She is mostly ignored by everyone except Prince Litaviccos."

"And you say he's been good to her?" Mary inquires.

Dummacos laughs. "He follows her like a puppy. No man could love Sarah more than him."

"I'm glad she has some happiness in her life. She deserves that much."

"One thing puzzles me," Dummacos interrupts. "I don't see a lot of you in her. She kind of has your eyes, but nothing of your face."

"Well captain, I can tell you with all honesty that she takes after her father far more than she takes after me."

"I thought that was the case," Dummacos musses and Mary laughs to herself.

"I must say you've treated me well for someone who tried to kill me," Mary says changing the subject.

"I wish I could make that up to you. But I know there is little I can say that will cause you to forgive me."

"Captain," Mary begins to say and then pauses. "What do your friends call you?"

"I don't have many. But the ones I do have call me 'Dros'," Dummacos replies.

"Well, Dros," Mary continues, "I don't suppose you have any daughters, do you?"

"I had two daughters," Dummacos says sadly.

"Had?" Mary inquires. "What happened?"

"It was during the last of the great raids on my clan. I was off fighting in a war and a group of bandits raided our village. They killed my wife, my son and my two daughters."

"I'm sorry. How old were they?"

"My son was sixteen. He was of age and would soon join the fighting. My daughters were eleven and five."

"Did you ever find the ones responsible?"

"They were already dead by the time I came home. They had been killed in a neighboring raid. If they had hit that clan first, maybe my daughters would still be alive."

There is a silence and then Mary says, "I guess I should take solace in the fact that Sarah is still alive."

"I don't know what is worse," Dummacos says. "Having your family taken from you, but knowing that they are finally safe from this war and pain. Or, having them alive, but not being able to see them... touch them."

"Either way, there is always hope that you will see them again. Either here or on the other side."

"How can you be so sure?" Dummacos asks with desperation in his voice.

"Because someone I trust taught me to believe. It seems like a very long time ago," Mary says with a smile. There is a long pause. "Dros?" Mary whispers.

"Yes?"

"What would you have done to save your daughters?"

"I would have given my life." Dummacos replies.

"What would you be willing to do to save my daughter?" Mary asks cautiously.

"You mean to see you and Princess Sarah safely out of Gaul?" Dummacos asks in lower tones.

"Yes," Mary whispers desperately.

"I've thought of that on several occasions," Dummacos admits.

"You have?" Mary asks surprised. "Will you help me?" she says as anticipation lifts her spirit and she rises to her knees.

"I cannot," Dummacos drops his head and sighs. All of Mary's anticipation escapes like a torrent flood from her body and she slumps back down to the ground where she was sitting. "It is not that I am unwilling," Dummacos continues. "I have mulled plan after plan through my mind. At times, I can think of nothing else. The problem is that I can't do it alone. There are too many men stationed here that are too loyal to Vercingetorix. No matter which direction we could go, the risk of being caught is too great. And, if we tried to take Sarah, Litaviccos would never let her go for any reason. And he wouldn't leave his father."

"Even if his father is the monster?" Mary quips.

"Litaviccos has no idea what kind of man his father is. Vercingetorix is a very manipulative man. He only lets the prince see what he wants him to see. Litaviccos thinks of his father as an outstanding king… a true hero to his people. That's what's so funny about how Sarah treats him. Vercingetorix has had a much harder time trying to control her. I laugh at his complaints about her. Not to his face… naturally. But behind his back."

"Is there no hope of escape?" Mary sighs longingly.

"There is always hope," Dummacos smiles. "You taught me that." Mary doesn't say anything. "Patience. Just a little longer. There will be an opportunity… I feel it in my bones."

"What will happen to me if there is not?"

"I do not know. But I will not let Vercingetorix harm you. You have my word on that."

"But you are only a soldier. How can you promise that?"

"Because I have fallen in love with you, Mary. No harm will come to you as long as I still have breath." Mary is shocked by the response and finds herself speechless, and somehow frightened. She gets up and quickly retreats back down the tunnel. "Mary?" Dummacos calls out hearing the movement. He gets up to peek around the corner but she is already gone. He shakes his head dejectedly, picks up the stool and walks back to his men.

Mary collapses on her bed with her heart racing. "How could he love me?" she thinks. "I don't want him to love me. I just want to use him to get Sarah and leave this place. I don't want love... I didn't ask for love." Her mind races and a flood of emotion comes over her and she plops her head down on the bed and begins to cry.

"Why do you cry, Mary?" comes a voice. Mary looks up and wipes at her eyes. It is the same messenger that had come to her before. The messenger holds out her hand and Mary rises from the bed. She walks over to the angel and grabs hold of her hand. "Why do you cry?" the messenger asks again.

"I'm confused," Mary pleads. "I don't know what's going to happen to me or Sarah and the man I was going to use to get us out of here just told me that he loves me. Is it possible that after all this, I might love him too? No! I can't! It's impossible. Tell me what to do. How do I escape here?"

"Calm yourself, Mary. Breathe deeply and close your eyes." The messenger says in a mesmerizing voice. Mary stifles her tears and takes a few deep breathes. She closes her eyes and a soothing calm washes over her whole body. "Now, open your eyes," the messenger says. Mary opens her eyes and there is nothing but a white void around her. The angel no longer glows and looks like a normal woman.

"What is this place?" Mary asks. "Where am I? Is this heaven?"

The messenger drops Mary's hand and says, "Yes... and no." This time the sound comes from her voice as she speaks the words.

"I don't understand," Mary says.

The messenger waves her hand and a golden path appears before Mary. "This is a vision, Mary. It is part heaven and part not. But do not concern yourself about that. Just follow this path."

With some trepidation Mary begins down the path and the messenger disappears. The white void is replaced with a view of the palace far below the path. It startles Mary and she freezes momentarily. She feels like she might fall from the path and plummet several hundred feet to the ground below. After a few moments, she timidly puts one foot in front of the other and continues down the path. After a few steps, her courage returns and she continues slowly walking. The palace fades away and is replaced by celebration all around her. She sees the wedding and sees Sarah dancing and hears her say, "I wish mama was here. I miss her." As she reaches out to Sarah, the scene disappears. As she walks further, she sees Dummacos sitting at night, all alone by a campfire, pleading to "the God of Mary" for forgiveness for what he has done to her. For a moment her heart is warmed and she feels a blush in her cheeks. She reaches to touch him. Then she is startled by the loud noise of a scream. She turns to see the image of Sarah's face scrunched in agony and screaming in pain. It wrenches Mary's body as she cries out to Sarah and reaches to touch a face that fades. As the image continues, the pain is from labor as she gives birth to a child and Mary can see the infant in Sarah's arms. The scene changes once more and she's now high in the air again. She sees armies massing on great plains below. She sees massive battles all around the path as she now seems to be among the fighting. She covers her ears and cowers as gruesome screams cry out and death is being inflicted all around her. She turns around and around as she inches along and sees men and women tortured and burned at stakes as they scream and writhe. Just when she thinks she can take no more, it all stops. Mary slowly removes her hands from her ears and stands up straight and all that exists is the path and the silence of the void. She can hear her heart beating inside her chest and begins to be afraid. "Mary," a familiar voice comes to her. She turns and sees a very familiar figure standing on the path. Without fear she now runs and embraces the figure. "Jesus, my Jesus. Is it really you?" Mary pulls back to look into his eyes.

"It is me," Jesus replies with a smile.

"I have missed you so much," Mary cries as she hugs him again. He strokes her hair as he hugs her tightly.

"I have missed you too," he says. He pushes her away and grabs her hand. "Let's walk." They begin to walk down the path again but it now meanders through an open field outside Jerusalem. Mary can see the outer wall and the top of the temple.

"I don't understand," Mary says. "Have I died? Is this heaven?"

"No," Jesus assures her. "Not yet. This is just a dream."

"Then it is a good dream." Mary says as she relaxes. "Those images I saw, have they come to pass?"

"Some have. Some are yet to be."

"What about Sarah? Will she be alright? Will I ever see her again?"

"Rest your troubled thoughts, Mary. Sarah will be fine. Things are in motion in which she will play a large part."

"Will I see her again?" Mary asks once more.

Jesus seems to hesitate. Then he says, "Before you leave this earth to be with me forever, you will see her again. I promise." This makes Mary smile. "But, you cannot interfere with what is to be done."

"Then let me stay. If I am of no more use to her, let me come home. Now. I do not want to be without you one day longer."

"Patience, Mary, my love. I did not say you had no part to play in this. Your time is not over. You still have love to share. There is a man waiting for you. One that will shape Sarah's fate as well as yours."

"But I have not loved any other man. I could not betray my love for you."

"Mary, my earthly love for you is over. My love for you now is... different. You cannot understand it yet. But it is more complete than it could ever be on earth. Someday, you will love me again in the same way I love you. But for now, follow your heart and do not be afraid to love another."

"I have to go back?" Mary asks sadly.

Jesus draws her to him and kisses her. "With this kiss I give you the strength to endure a little longer. I will see you soon."

Mary reaches for him but everything turns back to the white void. "Mary," a voice comes once more. Mary turns and it is the messenger. "Take my hand," the messenger says. Mary reaches out and grabs the hand. "Now, open your eyes, Mary."

Mary's eyes pop open and her body raises up as she gasps. She is sitting in her bed. She looks around and nothing appears out of the ordinary. She rubs her face and gets up to walk over to the washbowl. She splashes her face with water and wonders about all that she has seen.

THE UNEXPECTED SURPRISE

Litaviccos comes into the room and finds Sarah already seated at the table. Most of the lights have been extinguished and only the four candles on the table light the small dining room. There is a servant waiting to seat him as he makes his way to the table. After Litaviccos is seated, the servant exits to make way for others now bringing food to the table.

"Oh, this is romantic," Litaviccos says teasingly

"It's been awhile since we've dined alone," Sarah replies. "I just wanted you all to myself tonight."

"Well, you have me."

"Do you require anything else, my lady? My lord?" asks one of the servants after the food has been placed.

"No, I'll ring if we require anything else," Litaviccos says.

"Enjoy!" says the servant as he bows and departs closing the door behind him.

"This looks very good," Litaviccos says as he turns his attention back to Sarah. The two of them begin to eat. "I'm so glad you did this. I get so tired of eating in the grand dining room. Having to sit there and listen to my father talk on and on... pretending to pay attention... Then he gets into the same old war stories over and over..." Sarah laughs. "You think it's funny," Litaviccos continues, "But if you or mother nod off, it's fine because you aren't supposed to care what battle took place when or which palace got taken." Sarah laughs again. "But I will be king one day – and I have to look like I care."

"Well, you're my husband tonight. Talk about what you want to talk about." There is a long pause while both of them chew. "Well," Sarah inquires, "what do you want to talk about?"

"I don't know, I'm thinking about it," demands Litaviccos. Sarah laughs despite trying to hold it back. "Ok princess-know-it-all," Litaviccos continues, "let's talk about you."

"Me?" Sarah asks shocked.

"Yes. How are you feeling? Better today?"

"About the same," Sarah says calmly

"Really?" Litaviccos says as he stops eating. "Because you look better."

"Do I?"

"Yes. Your eyes… It's something in your eyes. I don't think I've ever seen them so lovely."

"It's the candlelight. It makes you see things." Sarah say as she places her hand on top of his as it rests on the table.

"Maybe," Litaviccos smiles as he returns to his meal. "In any case, the physician should have come today to see you."

"He did. He told me exactly what was wrong with me," Sarah says nonchalantly.

"Oh? What did he say the issue was? Nothing serious I hope."

"I'm with child," Sarah says without looking up from her food. There is a loud clang as Litaviccos's fork and knife bounce off the metal plate. The door opens and a servant begins to come in. Litaviccos looks up and says, "No! Not now!" and the servant beats a hasty retreat. He turns to Sarah and asks, "With child?"

"Yes," Sarah beams. "Your child."

Litaviccos is speechless as his mouth begins several sentences, but no sound comes out. Finally, he manages to ask, "When? When will it come?"

Sarah says, "Midwinter." Litaviccos gets up and kneels by Sarah. She turns her chair to face him. Litaviccos places his head gently against her stomach and hugs her. Sarah wraps her arms around his head and lays her head on top of his.

"Me… a father…" Litaviccos mummers. He pulls back and looks up at Sarah, "Will it be a boy?"

Sarah giggles, "I don't know, silly. I'll know when he or she gets here."

Sarah storms past the guard's half-hearted attempt to stop her advance, preceded by her basketball like womb, as she stomps through the door. "Sarah, I told you I'm too busy today, can't we talk about this later?" Vercingetorix asks as he sits at his desk writing.

"You're always too busy," Sarah says angrily. "You were busy yesterday! You were busy all last week! You were busy all last month!"

"That doesn't change the fact that I'm busy now," Vercingetorix says without looking at her.

"I want to see my mother. It's been seven months."

"I'm only following her instructions." Vercingetorix says mechanically.

"But if she knew about the baby, she would return. I know she would."

"I told you I sent a messenger to tell her. She knows but she is still afraid for you. She will not come back."

"I don't believe you!" Sarah demands.

Vercingetorix looks up for a moment and then yells, "Guards!" The guards come in and gingerly try to grab at Sarah's arms. She wrestles them lose before they actually have a hold. She gives Vercingetorix one last deadly stare and then stomps out of the room.

When Litaviccos comes into the bedroom, Sarah is sitting on the bed waiting on him.

"Don't give me that look, Sarah. I cannot control what my father does."

"Something is wrong. Mama would not stay hidden this long. He's hiding something."

Litaviccos goes to the side of the bed to hug Sarah but she will not let him. She continues to glare at him as he says sheepishly, "I don't know. It does seem strange that you can't go see her."

"It's more than strange. Something is wrong."

"Calm down. You have to think of the baby."

"The baby is fine." Sarah says in a calmer tone.

"I don't know about that. I'm afraid he'll come out screaming, 'It's more than strange. Something is wrong! I'm cold and naked!'" Sarah lets out a chuckle and then quickly suppresses it. She looks up at Litaviccos and slaps at him.

"Stop that!" Sarah demands.

"Stop what?"

"Stop making me laugh. I want to stay mad right now." She looks at him with a pout face which makes him almost laugh. She then lays her head on his chest and wraps her arms around him while they sit on the bed. "I'm scared, Vio. Something is wrong and mama is in danger. I feel it. I only want to see her again."

"I know," Litaviccos says as he rubs her back. "I may have to go around my father..."

Sarah jerks back and excitedly asks, "Will you? For me?"

Litaviccos pulls her back to him, "It could be dangerous, but I'll see what I can find out. But you have to stay out of father's way, please?"

The Journey of Mary Magdalene

"Well... At least for a little while, I promise. I love you!"

Dummacos and Mary sit in their usual places at the cave entrance. It has become the daily exercise in passing a good part of the day. Dummacos has started letting others serve Mary food to hide the amount of time he spends talking to her, but it's a vain effort as their relationship is the subject of the guard's conversations held in Dummacos' absences.

"One of my men came in this morning," Dummacos says. "Sarah has not delivered yet."

"She must be getting close," Mary says concerned. She then coughs a deep cough.

"Your cough is getting worse."

"No, it's about the same," Mary scoffs. "It the cold and the damp together. I just haven't gotten used to it."

"I told Vercingetorix I needed to bring a physician out here last time I was at the palace," explains Dummacos. "He just ignored me. I should have brought one anyway."

"I'll be fine, don't worry."

"But I do worry about you, Mary," Dummacos says, but then quickly adds, "I'm sorry."

"Don't be, Dros," Mary mutters. "I haven't been totally honest with you lately."

"What is it?" Dummacos asks with peaked interest.

"It seems that I do have feeling for you, Dros." Mary confesses.

"You do not know how glad that makes my heart," Dummacos says with a great sigh. "I have loved you for so long. I have prayed to God, as you have taught me, that he might unharden your heart to me."

"I too have been praying," Mary replies, "but for the strength to confess my love for you."

"Your love gives me the courage to tell you of my plan."

"What plan?" Mary asks through a coughing spell.

"I have a plan to sneak you and me out of the kingdom. I was unwilling to attempt it and put you in danger if we would never be together."

"What about Sarah?" Mary asks concerned.

"I cannot risk kidnapping the princess. The plan would not work. Even if she came willingly, the baby might not survive the trip." Mary doesn't respond. "Please, Mary. Let me save you so I can take you somewhere to make you better and we can spend the rest of our lives together."

"I cannot leave Sarah. I cannot explain why. It's too complicated," Mary says.

"As you wish, my love. But I will risk bringing a physician out here as soon as possible."

"I'm feeling a little weak. I'm going to go take a nap to recover my strength." She struggles to get up so Dummacos helps her and starts her down the tunnel. He grabs the stool and walks back towards the men with his head down, lost in thought and his concern building. He is met by two of his soldiers.

"Sir?" asks one of them.

Dummacos looks up and sees them. He stiffens up and asks, "What is it?"

The soldier hesitates and then stammers, "Sorry sir, but the men know you have feelings for Mary, and…"

"Do they?" Dummacos interrupts.

"Well, yes sir," the soldier continues, "and we think you should attempt it."

"What is that supposed to mean?" Dummacos asks sternly.

The two soldiers look at each other and the second one says, "We've been talking among ourselves… All the guys are loyal to you…"

"We know she's sick," the first one continues, "and we've come to care about her too. So, we can give you two horses and we can make sure that the report doesn't reach the palace for two days. That would give you time to make the Roman territory."

Dummacos snorts and smiles as his body relaxes, "Is it that obvious? You guys would do that for me?"

"Yes sir!" that both say.

"You've saved a lot of us through the years," says the first. "Most of us owe you our life. We've all agreed that we'd be willing to risk ourselves for this."

"Thanks," Dummacos says. "But she won't leave. I've already asked her." There is a long silence as they just look at each other.

"Well, at least go in there and look after her," the first one says.

"Yeah, go," the second one says. "Nothing leaves this camp about it."

"Tell the rest of the men their loyalty will not go unrewarded," Dummacos says and turns to go back to the entrance.

"Dros, what are you doing in here now?" Mary asks surprised.

"It appears our attempt to hide our feelings has failed miserably." Mary smiles. "So, they sent me in here to care for you. What can I do?"

"I'm fine," Mary says reassuring. As Dummacos sits on the side of the bed, she puts her hand up to his cheek and rubs his face. "I want you, Dros."

"What?" Dummacos asks in disbelief.

Mary smiles, "I want you, Dros. Now. Do you think you're up to it?"

Dummacos smiles.

The Gift

Litaviccos walks in to Viscount Gobannitio's room. He is Vercingetorix's lead advisor. He smiles at Litaviccos but doesn't immediately cease his work. As Litaviccos continues staring, Gobannitio finally asks dryly, "Is there something you want, Prince Litaviccos?"

"I didn't want to interrupt you if you were doing something important," Litaviccos says.

"Well, I am rather…"

"But I just had a question or two," Litaviccos interjects.

"Very well," Gobannitio sighs. "What do you want to know?"

"You've served my father since I can remember." Litaviccos says nonchalantly. "I guess you two are friends from way back."

"Yes. I remember the day you were born. You're father paced outside the room for hours."

"I know he loves me, but sometimes I wonder if he likes me. He never lets me do anything important."

"You were not the first born. You had an older brother." Gobannitio whispers.

"What? I didn't know that. What happen to him?"

"You were never supposed to know. Never tell anyone I told you that," pleads Gobannitio.

"Not a word," Litaviccos swears.

"He died during childbirth. Your father was devastated. It took years for him to know your mother again. That's probably why he protects and shields you so."

169

"But he doesn't trust me." Litaviccos says.

"Of course he trusts you," Gobannitio replies.

"He would not tell me where Mary is being hidden."

Gobannitio looks nervously towards the door and whispers, "Please, Prince Litaviccos. Never speak of that."

"Why? What is father hiding?"

"I can't tell you. It would mean my life. It's something that you would be better off not knowing anything about."

"But Sarah must know where she is," Litaviccos pleads.

"No!" Gobannitio shoos Litaviccos out of the room. "Go now. And never bring it up again. Go, I have work to do."

"That scream was more blood-curdling than the last one." Litaviccos stands outside the door wringing his hands and pacing. "How much more can she take?" Litaviccos wonders. The door swings open and a midwife walks out to head up the hallway. Even though it's obvious she's in a hurry, Litaviccos asks, "What news?"

"No difference than it was ten minutes ago when you asked me, my prince," the midwife says disparagingly.

"Is there anything I can do?" Litaviccos asks.

"Yes, my prince," says the midwife. "Stop stopping me every time I come out the door." She then walks quickly up the hallway and around the corner. Vercingetorix comes around the same corner and sees his son standing there. As he strolls past his son, a slow rolling laugh develops and continues until Vercingetorix turns the next corner. "What?" Litaviccos wonders.

Another long scream builds and ends. "That one didn't seem as loud as the last one," Litaviccos thinks. The midwife returns with a stack of folded cloths and ducks quickly through the door. Litaviccos tries to catch a glimpse of Sarah but cannot see anything of consequence.

It's been four hours, but for Litaviccos it seems like twenty. He begins to pace again. There is another very long scream. "That one was much louder," Litaviccos thinks.

But the next sound Litaviccos hears is that of a baby crying. "It's over," Litaviccos thinks. "It's finally over." He staggers over to a bench in the hallway and plops down. He stares at the door breathing heavily and waiting for it to open. Any second. Waiting. Waiting…

"What's taking so long?" Litaviccos wonders. The baby is here. I heard it. What else is there left to do? Why haven't they opened the door?" Litaviccos stands back up and begins to pace again. "What if something went wrong?" he thinks. "What if there's bad news? Maybe that's why they haven't let me in. But I'm the prince. I should be able to go in if I want to." He walks over to the door but hesitates grabbing the knob. "Should I go in? Maybe I should wait. But why?" Just as he's about to grab the knob, the door swings open and he stands face to face with the midwife. Litaviccos feels embarrassed but the midwife just smiles and says, "Come in, my prince."

Litaviccos rushes in and goes to the bed where Sarah is laying covered with sheets and kneels down. "Are you alright?" he asks gingerly.

Sarah places her hand on his face. "Of course. I'm just fine now," she says beaming.

"I was so worried…" Litaviccos begins to say.

"My prince," one of the midwives interrupts, "here is your son."

Litaviccos stands and turns, "My son?" He gazes upon the little baby bundled in a blanket in the arms of the midwife. "My son," he repeats. "He's beautiful. Is he healthy? Is there anything wrong…"

"He's perfect, my prince." Interrupts the midwife.

Litaviccos sits down on the bed and kisses Sarah. "He perfect. Did you hear that?"

Sarah laughs, "Yes."

One of the midwives pulls Litaviccos up by the arm. "Alright, my prince. There are a few more things which we must do and then we will be done." She leads him to the door. "They're both fine. Go and do some prince stuff and come back later."

Sarah laughs softly, "Go, and I'll send someone for you when I'm ready." Litaviccos is pushed out the door and it is closed behind him leaving him standing in the hallway a bit dazed. "Yes," he thinks to himself. "I will go do some prince stuff."

Litaviccos walks into the kitchen in a daze while the kitchen servants rush about trying to prepare for the next meal. Leeda is an elderly woman who has worked in the kitchen for years. She always had a treat for Litaviccos when he was a small boy and would come into the kitchen after playing outside. She approaches Litaviccos and asks, "Is the baby here yet?"

"Yes," Litaviccos says as he snaps out of his daze. "I have a son! How are you today, Leeda?"

"Congratulations, my prince. I'm as good as ever. Can I make you a snack?"

"No. I'm just… ah…" Litaviccos stammers.

"You're just what?" smiles Leeda.

"I'm just doing some prince stuff." Litaviccos says confidently.

"Oh, I see. What kind of prince stuff?"

"Well, one thing I'm trying to do is find out where Mary is, but no one will tell me." Leeda suddenly becomes very nervous looking. "What is it, Leeda? What do you know?"

After looking around, she pulls Litaviccos into a corner of the kitchen. "I should not tell you this. Please don't tell anyone I told you," Leeda whispers.

"No one," Litaviccos swears. "Do you know where she is?"

"No. But I have made her some special food to be taken to where she is. And anytime I make something, I'm told by the soldiers that no one can know what I'm making, especially the king. When I asked why, the soldiers told me that they were sneaking food in to her and I'd be in trouble if anybody knew."

"That's strange," Litaviccos scratches his head. "Why all the secrecy about her food?"

"If the king was hiding her, I would think she could have anything she wanted to eat. Something's not right, if you ask me," Leeda nods. Then looking around says, "I've got to get the meal ready. Don't tell anybody what I told you." She scurries off to continue her work.

"Not a word," Litaviccos whispers after her.

That evening, Litaviccos sits next to Sarah who sits in a chair rocking the baby. "He looks like you," Sarah says.

"Too bad," Litaviccos teases.

Sarah looks at him with shock. "What do you mean? You are the most handsome man in the kingdom. He will be the most handsome prince this kingdom has ever known."

"A mother's prejudice," Litaviccos laughs.

"I am the princess. My opinion is the only one that matters," Sarah laughs back.

"I feel like a very lucky man tonight, Sarah," Litaviccos sighs as he lightly rubs the baby's head with his finger

"I am the lucky one," Sarah muses. "I've come so far in such a short life." Then after a short pause, "So Vio, what is his name, my prince?"

"I guess we should have spent more time talking about that. We might have picked one by now."

"Well, we did decide on a girl's name," Sarah says. "But the boy's name I thought you liked was Calix."

"Yes, I did like that name. What about you?"

"I think Calix is a wonderful name. It's a Latin name and all the babies are being named in Latin now… it's perfect."

"Very well," Litaviccos says in a deep voice like he is announcing it to the world, "the new prince shall be named Prince Calix."

"Did you ever find out about my mother?" Sarah asks.

"I'm getting closer. I'm beginning to suspect that you may be right. My father may be hiding something."

"What?" Sarah asks. "It's nothing bad, is it?"

"I don't know. I asked several of father's advisors, but none of them knew anything."

"None of them?"

"Until I asked Gobannitio. He knows something. I don't know what, and he wouldn't tell me. He said it was better if we didn't know."

"So what now?" Sarah sighs.

"I don't know. All I've found are roads to nowhere."

"You have to keep trying," Sarah pleads.

"Yes, I will. But it could be dangerous for us if my father finds out we are undermining his authority… We must be careful." Sarah nods. After kissing his son on the head, Litaviccos says, "It's getting late. You aren't going to stay all night with him, are you?"

THE AMBUSH

The door opens and Captain Dummacos walks into the room. "Captain! Just the man I've been waiting for. It's about time you got here," Vercingetorix says as he drops his quill and rises from the desk.

"I'm sorry, my lord. I came from the cave as soon as I received your summons" Dummacos says as he walks to the desk.

"Of course you did. How is our brave Mary doing?" Vercingetorix asks callously.

"She still has a bad cough. It's getting worse. That cave is too damp. I still think she needs a physician."

"Well, it's a good thing I don't pay you to think then, isn't captain?" Vercingetorix snaps.

"My lord?" Dummacos says confused. "You told me to keep her alive."

"I said I didn't want her killed," Vercingetorix muses as he begins to pace back and forth. "But, if she were to die of natural causes, her secret would be forever safe and I'm off the hook."

"What secret, my lord?"

"Oh," Vercingetorix says disgruntled that he had let that slip, "never mind that. It's not important."

"I don't think we should let her die this soon," Dummacos argues.

"Excuse me, captain, but did I just here the word *think* escape from your lips twice in the same conversation?" Vercingetorix says sarcastically.

"Sorry, my lord."

"We have complications which I did not foresee." Vercingetorix continues.

"Complications?"

"That pesky Sarah won't leave me alone. She's insistent on seeing her mother and now, I find out that my own son is now trying to go around my authority, behind my back, to find out where she is."

"She has great sway on the prince."

"Yes. That is what worries me most. It's not enough for him to simple keep her as a wife. He's so love-struck with her that he's becoming weak. He's forgetting his place as my heir and letting that woman have her way with him. She will drive him to ruin all because she can't get over her mama. That is why I called for you."

"What would you have me do, my lord?"

Vercingetorix continues to pace. "She's given my son a legitimate heir to the Jewish grip I've created. I am going to send her with my son on a diplomatic mission. But, unfortunately, Princess Sarah will meet an untimely end at the hands of the Romans, just like her mother should have."

Dummacos's heart sinks. He asks hesitantly, "You want me to kill Princess Sarah?"

Vercingetorix stops in front of Dummacos and gets close to his face. "Do you really think I want you to botch this job like you did with the mother? I'm out of caves, captain," Vercingetorix snaps. He then begins to pace again and speaks out to no one in particular. "I will handle this myself. It must be done in total secrecy to work. Besides, it will give me a certain amount of pleasure to put an end to all that ceaseless yapping. You will accompany them to make sure that she gets to a designated spot for an ambush…" Vercingetorix stops and walks over to the desk. He grabs a parchment and unrolls it on the desktop. He begins to search the map on the parchment as Dummacos draws close to the desk. "But where?"

Dummacos snaps his finger down on the map, "Here! It's far enough from the palace and it's a good place for an ambush. The hills here are steep and my men would be defenseless to stop you."

"Yes. A good choice, captain," Vercingetorix nods. "When you get there, stop so you can separate Litaviccos and Sarah. I don't want to accidentally hit my son. You will bring her there and *I* will kill her." Vercingetorix paces once more. "I can't trust any of your men to keep that kind of secret. I will kill her in a way that I can pin it on the Romans as well. She is so much more popular than her mother, not to mention being a princess now. The kingdom will be simply outraged. Of course, I regret the inconvenience it will cause Litaviccos, but it just can't be helped. He seems to genuinely care for this one... probably because it's his first. I seem to remember having feeling for my first wife – his mother. But I got over it and he will too. It won't be long before he finds another wife or two to give him more children. We will have such a wake that it will cement my power over the Jews in this part of the world for ever. Maybe the Jews all over the world, who knows?" Vercingetorix laughs. He looks at Dummacos, who is not laughing, and his laughter suddenly fades. Vercingetorix walks back to his desk. "I will need the week to plan out all the details and I will get back to you. I will then leave alone to 'spy on one of my governors'. That will establish my alibi. The next day, you will bring her to me."

"As you wish, my lord," Dummacos says as he heads for the door.

"And captain," Vercingetorix says in a sinister tone and Dummacos stops and turns. "I've given you something very simple this time. Do not fail me again."

"I know what I must do. I will not fail," Dummacos says as he slowly turns and exits the room.

Sarah and Litaviccos are talking in their favorite garden as Sarah cuddles with her new son. Vercingetorix enters and asks, "Am I interrupting?"

"No, father. Please." Litaviccos says as he motions his father closer.

"I am in need of your service," Vercingetorix begins, "actually the both of you."

"What do you need?" Litaviccos asks.

"I have a pressing issue which I must attend to personally. But I was also scheduled to meet with King Bituitus in four days. I think he wants to impress me with something, though the message didn't say. So, I'm going to send you and Sarah in my place."

"I don't understand, father," Litaviccos shakes his head.

"This is a diplomatic visit. You are more than old enough to start fulfilling your role as heir to the throne. Simple go see him, represent our interests, see whatever he has for you and then come home."

"Very well, I will go in your stead and make you proud."

"That's my boy. Start making a name for yourself." Turning to Sarah, he says, "You must also go. I want to show off my newest prince."

"Of course I will go if you wish it. It will be good to see King Bituitus again. He is such a great king to his people," Sarah says coldly

Trying hard to ignore her, Vercingetorix smiles and says to Litaviccos, "Thank you. You're really helping me out of a mess. Captain Dummacos will escort you there. I've left instructions with him." Vercingetorix and Sarah exchange a quick, hateful stare and then Vercingetorix makes a quick exit as Litaviccos watches him leave and then chuckles.

"What is it, Vio?" Sarah asks.

"This is the first thing he's ever asked me to do outside of the palace. I can't believe I finally get to do something," Litaviccos says gleefully.

Sarah smiles and whispers to her son, "We get to go on our first trip with papa."

"But," Litaviccos says with a deep breath, "I do wish that you would not antagonize him like that."

"Whatever do you mean?" Sarah asks innocently. Litaviccos just sighs and shakes his head.

Vercingetorix climbs up onto his horse. He is dressed as a common man of meager means. "My lord, are you sure you don't want me send a few soldiers with you," Dummacos asks, as he plays his part while Sarah and Litaviccos look on.

"Captain Dummacos is right, father," says Litaviccos. "You should not try this alone."

"I just want to check on the activities of one of my governors with my own eyes. No one will know I'm there. And besides, we're at peace. It's not like I'm going into battle."

"But father," Litaviccos interrupts.

"I did not get to be king without being able to look after myself," Vercingetorix snaps.

"Let me come with you, then," Litaviccos suggests.

"I need you to take my place and leave tomorrow. We've already discussed it."

"Of course," Litaviccos says, "I won't let you down."

"That's my boy. I'll be back within a week. I promise," Vercingetorix says as he spurs his horse on towards the palace gate.

On the morning of the next day, Captain Dummacos stands with his horse next to three mounted soldiers. Litaviccos and Sarah emerge from the palace followed by a nursemaid holding her son.

"Good morning, captain," Litaviccos tries to say as officially as he can.

"How are you feeling, my prince?" Dummacos asks pleasantly.

"Can I be honest with you?" Litaviccos mumbles. Dummacos nods. "I'm a little nervous, captain. This is my first time to go outside of the palace. Well, representing my father that is."

"I would not worry," Dummacos says dryly. "I have a feeling you will be up to the task of this day."

Litaviccos and Sarah enter an open carriage while the nursemaid takes the baby into a smaller covered carriage. Dummacos mounts his horse and orders the entourage forward and the carriages lurch as they begin to move towards the palace gate. That same morning, Vercingetorix wakes up as the sun dawns. He spends the morning examining several spots in which he can stand or crouch and put an arrow through the princess without being seen and then escape quickly. Not that he has too much to worry about, because Dummacos will coral the soldiers if they get to ambitious. He refreshes the campfire and cooks some of the meat he brought with him for lunch. He plays the shot over and over in his mind. He begins to plan the funeral and grins when he thinks of the how much the people will be outraged. It will only be another hour or two. He is lost in thought when his trance is broken with,

"Well, well, well. What do we have here?" He grabs for his sword, stands up and spins around ready to attack. He sees four scraggly bandits. They have no armor, but are all armed with an assortment of weapons. Some are slightly rusty, but look sturdy enough.

"What are you doing here?" Vercingetorix demands.

"This is our land. Anybody who camps here has to pay us," says the leader menacingly.

"Really?" Vercingetorix says haughtily. "And how much would that be?"

"How much have you got?" says another and the group begins to laugh.

"Look, you better clear out, or I'll have your heads," demands Vercingetorix.

"He sounds dangerous, Buk," says one. "Maybe we should just take all his stuff and run."

"Ok," the leader says, "Strip down and give us all your stuff and we'll consider not killing you."

Vercingetorix begins to circle as they surround him and draw closer. "Look! This is your last warning," says Vercingetorix. "If any of you lay a hand on me, I will see you all hanged."

"And what makes you think you can do that?" another asks.

"Because... I am King Vercingetorix and I have an army coming up that valley anytime now."

"You don't say," says the leader. "I think I'd like to see that."

"No, I *am* the king... you can't touch me."

"But I'm the Roman Emperor..." the leader replies. "Kill him!"

As the first man lunges at Vercingetorix with a short sword, Vercingetorix parries and run him through. The bandit begins to fall over and Vercingetorix attempts to pull out his sword. But one of the bandits sinks his longsword between Vercingetorix's ribs before he can turn completely to parry. Vercingetorix does bring his sword through and slices the man's arm open and he drops the sword. The leader jumps in and stabs him through the back with a dagger and Vercingetorix falls to the ground. He lays in the dirt bleeding, with a burning in his lower body, and his life quickly seeping away. The three gather around him and look down.

"Really," Vercingetorix gasps, "I am the king. You have to spare me."

"No you're not…" the leader says. He raises the dagger and slams it down into Vercingetorix's heart. With a few jerks, the last of his breath escapes him and Vercingetorix's body is still. "Otherwise," the leader says as he pulls the dagger out, "I would have enjoyed that a whole lot more." The company begins to laugh.

"But Buk, this guy killed Shorty," says one bandit as the laughter subsides pointing to their dead comrade.

The leader stands up and says, "Shame. But it means more for the rest of us." And the trio breaks out in laughter again.

As they reach the edge of a glade, Dummacos advances to one of the soldiers and says, "Watch over the prince and princess. I'm going to go scout the area ahead and make sure it's safe." He urges his horse into a gallop and speeds ahead to check out the situation.

The lead bandit is patching up the man with the bleeding arm while the third rummages through the spoils.

"He's got plenty of food," says the third.

"That's good," the leader says. "Maybe we'll eat decent for a few days. There, that'll hold your arm until we can get it stitched up proper."

The third one begins to load the food into bags. After the leader patches up the one with the cut, he begins to help the third one go through what is around the camp. The second one, with the injured arm, begins to examine the body.

"Should we take the horse?" the leader asks.

"The face looks too distinctive. It'll get us caught," says the third.

"I agree," says the second.

"Means we'll have to carry all this stuff ourselves," says the leader.

"And how would that be different than any other day?" asks the second.

"Just saying," the leader replies.

The second bandit begins to examine the ring on Vercingetorix's hand as he tries to pull it off. A sudden panic comes over him and he drops the arm and jumps away from the body. "What's your problem?" asks the leader. The second bandit's forehead begins to bead with sweat and he begins to whimper uncontrollably. The leader drops what he has and walks over, grabs the shirt of the second and shakes him, "What is the matter with you?"

"That ring he has on," he says with a whimper, "that's the king's seal."

"What?" asks the leader skeptically. He walks over to the body and begins to examine the ring.

"That's the king's seal." The second bandit says again.

"And how would you know that?" asks the third as he stops scrounging.

"I've seen it on the death decree of my father. He was hanged by the king."

"I think you may be right," the leader says nervously. "I think he was telling the truth. I think this was the king." He drops the arm and stands away.

"We've killed King Vercingetorix?" the third one yells.

"Shut up!" replies the leader. "Let's not panic."

"Not panic?" cries the third. "Do you know how many people will be searching for us?"

"There's nowhere in Gaul for us to hide," says the second. "We're all dead men."

"Just shut up while I think," yells the leader.

His thought is cut short by the sound of a sword being pulled from the sheath. All three bandits freeze as they look up and see Captain Dummacos standing on the ridge with sword drawn. There is a long silence as he eyes each of them and then walks a few steps to see the body of Vercingetorix lying in the grass in a pool of blood. He raises his sword and with a quick stroke stabs it into the ground.

"A job well done, gentlemen," Dummacos says casually.

"Well done?" stammers the leader. "I think we've killed the king!"

"That you have."

"You didn't tell us he was the king when you hired us."

"Would you have killed him if I had told you that he was the king?"

"No! Of course not."

"That's why I didn't tell you."

"You don't understand. You've made us marked men. They won't stop searching the entire kingdom... all of Gaul... until they find us."

"And then they won't kill us," squeals the third, "until after they've tortured us for days..."

"Then you'll have to leave Gaul," Dummacos calmly replies. The bandits stand stunned.

"And just how do we accomplish that?" the leader asks angrily. "You only gave us 40 silver. That won't get us to the borders of Celtica. We'll have to bribe a lot of people to get out of Gaul."

"Then you'll need more," Dummacos says as he heaves a medium sized pouch towards them. The leader catches it and dumps some of the coins into his hands.

"This is gold," the leader says stunned.

"Enough to get you all the way to the Roman sea and beyond, if you're careful." The three start to chuckle as they eye the gold. The other two run over to touch it. "But, the king's men are headed this way and they will probably find his body in about two hours, so the sooner you leave the better chance you have to outrun them."

"He's right," the leader says snapping back to the situation. "Take the horse! We won't be stopping at any towns!" The other two jump into action, but then curiosity gets the best of the leader and he asks, "Just who are you, anyway?"

Dummacos smiles, "Oh, just your everyday Roman soldier doing what needed to be done." The leader just stares at him with a puzzled look until he is urged to hurry by the other two. There is mad scramble by the bandits to load up the horse with supplies and Dummacos, after replacing his sword and tossing a couple more logs onto the campfire, turns and walks away.

WHAT WAS LOST IS FOUND

One of the soldiers rides up next to the carriage. He points to the distance, "My prince, Captain Dummacos returns." Soon Dummacos rejoins the group.

"Did you see anything, captain?" Litaviccos calls out.

"Nothing surprising. Everything was just as I expected it to be." Dummacos replies and takes his place at the head of the convoy.

After traveling almost an hour and a half, one of the other soldiers says, "Captain, look." He points off into the distance. "I see smoke rising."

"Hmm," Dummacos muses. "I don't remember seeing that when I came through. It's probably nothing but a huntsman's campfire. Still, with the prince and princess in tow, we should make sure it's not thieves." He points out two of the soldiers, "Go check it out and be quiet about it. Just in case they're armed." With a nod, the two ride off up the hill towards the smoke. It isn't very long before a single rider comes galloping back towards the group. Dummacos stops the convoy and waits for the rider. As he approaches, Dummacos ask, "What news?"

"The young soldier looks panicked and mutters, "It's… it's the king… he's… he's dead, sir."

"What?" Dummacos reacts with a shocked tone. "The king? Here? Are you sure?"

"Yes sir. There is a dead… a dead bandit there also. He… ah, the king… he's cut up pretty bad."

Dummacos moves his horse closer to the carriage. "What is it?" Litaviccos asks.

"I'm afraid we're going to have to divert, Prince Litaviccos. This soldier thinks the king is up there on the hill, dead."

"Dead! My father, dead?" Litaviccos asks in disbelief.

"I don't understand how that could be. We will go check it out," Dummacos says. "This way," he orders and they turn towards where the smoke is rising. After reaching the foot of the hill, it is too steep for the carriage. Litaviccos and Sarah are put onto two horses of soldiers who will stay behind and guard the group and they follow Dummacos and three others up the hill. When they arrive at the camp, Litaviccos jumps off his horse to look at the body. He cries out when he realizes that it is the king. Sarah runs to his side as he stands numb in shock.

"My father is dead," Litaviccos mutters.

"I'm so sorry," Sarah tries to comfort him.

"What happened here, captain?" Litaviccos asks.

"It's bandits, my lord. Look at all the footprints. They killed your father; maybe kidnapped him and brought him here from somewhere else. When they saw us coming, they probably panicked and fled. That would explain why they didn't dowse the fire."

"Sir, there is more blood over here," says one of the soldiers.

"It looks like the king got in a few good strikes before he went down," Dummacos explains.

"Fresh horse tracks lead off this way," says another. "It's hard to tell just how old they are."

Dummacos turns to Litaviccos and asks, "My lord?" Litaviccos is unresponsive. He repeats it louder, "My lord!" Litaviccos snaps out of his stupor and looks at Dummacos. "What are your orders, my lord?" asks Dummacos.

"My orders?" Litaviccos asks dazed.

"Yes, you are now King Litaviccos," Dummacos says as he kneels to one knee. The rest of the soldiers take their cue and also kneel. Sarah stands stunned off to the side as she can do nothing but look on. Litaviccos takes a deep breath and he tries to steady himself. He quietly clears his throat and says, "Captain Dummacos, a word in private, please?"

"Of course, my lord" and he rises and walks with Litaviccos a few steps.

"Please, my head is spinning right now," Litaviccos whispers. "What would you do?"

"Well," Dummacos ponders, "first I'd order a group to go after these bandits. Second, I'd send a runner back to the palace for reinforcements. Third, we need take care of your father's body. And lastly, do not forget to claim the seal ring or your reign could be short lived; you know the tradition." After a moment he puts his hand on Litaviccos' shoulder and says solemnly, "You tried to warn him; we all did. There's nothing you can do about that now. There will be time to grieve later, but now you must be king."

"Thank you, captain. You are a true friend as well as a loyal protector."

"I assure you my lord, I will enjoy serving you even more than I did your father," Dummacos says with a small smile.

Litaviccos turns and walks back toward the soldiers. They are still kneeling and he says, "Oh, get up, already." As they are standing up, he goes over to his father's body and retrieves the seal ring from his finger. He puts on the ring in the sight of those assembled. "By my right to possess the seal of my clan," Litaviccos begins, "I *am* King Litaviccos." The soldiers cheer and raise their swords in support. "Captain, we need to chase down these bandits," he says loud enough for the rest to hear. "Send someone the palace to bring reinforcements to help in the pursuit. We need to take my father's body back to the palace."

"It will be done, my lord," says Dummacos with a wink. He begins to organize the soldiers and gets them moving. Lost in all of the unfolding story, Litaviccos finally notices Sarah standing off to the side, sobbing. He goes to be with her.

"What's troubling you?" Litaviccos asks.

"You father was the only one who knows where my mother is. How will I find her now?"

As Litaviccos takes her into his arms, Dummacos steps up and kneels. She turns her head as he says, "I couldn't help overhearing you, Princess... I mean, *Queen* Sarah. It's not true. I know where she is. Command me and I will take you to her."

"Yes, I command that." Sarah says with a sigh of relief as she pushes away from Litaviccos and hugs the kneeling Dummacos.

"Take care of his body," Litaviccos instructs a soldier. "When you get to the palace, tell Viscount Gobannitio that he is in charge of my father and to begin making arrangements. I'll return as soon as I can. And take good care of my son!"

"Yes, my lord," the soldier replies.

"Let's go, captain," Litaviccos says as he climbs into the carriage.

Dummacos spurs his horse and he and the carriage are off to the cave. On the way, Dummacos warns Sarah of Mary's medical condition. The guards are alerted to their approach, but when they see Dummacos, they stand down.

"She's in here?" Sarah asks.

"Yes," Dummacos replies and hands a torch to Litaviccos. He leads Litaviccos and Sarah to her bed where she lays semi-unconscious and barely breathing. Her face is ashen and she is cool to the touch. Dummacos moves to the far side and picks up Mary's hand between his two. Sarah appears to be the only one that notices. Sarah wrings a washcloth in a bucket of water next to the bed and lays it on her forehead. Mary makes a faint sound and her eyes slowly open.

"Mama?" Sarah pats her face. "Mama, can you hear me?"

"It's true," Mary whispers weakly. Sarah draws very close to hear. "My time is near, for now I have beheld you with my own eyes one more time."

"Mama, I'm going to bring you back to the palace," Sarah whispers.

"It's too late for that. There was a price for my sin, and now it has been paid to save you."

"Mama, don't say that. I'm going to save you from here," Sarah cries.

"Listen to me. Do not let your heart be troubled, my daughter. It is you who the Lord favors now. You and your son." She weakly reaches for Sarah's face. "There are so many things I've should have told you."

"I wanted you to see him... To hold him," Sarah says mournfully.

Mary smiles a weak smile. "I have seen him. The angel showed him to me. Jesus told me what would happen," Mary says as she is interrupted with a cough that shakes her whole body. "Do not forget the Lord. And do not cry for me. I am going home, now. We shall see each other again someday. But for now, be strong."

"No, mama," Sarah pleads, "not yet. Not yet..."

Mary looks at Dummacos and squeezes his hand with what strength she has left. There is one more large breath and then Mary's eyes close and her breathing stops. Sarah lays her head next to Mary's and begins to cry. Litaviccos kneels next to Sarah and wraps his arms around her as she cries. Dummacos places Mary's hand on the bed and stands in silence. Some time passes and Litaviccos pulls Sarah to her feet as he says, "Come, Sarah. Captain, please see to Mary so we can take her back."

"Of course, my lord," Dummacos replies. As Sarah stands and looks at Dummacos, she notices a single tear running down his cheek as well.

The three exit from the cave and the men are standing in a solemn arc with heavy hearts and heads hanging.

"Is she...?" asks one soldier.

Dummacos nods. There is a collective sigh. "And I bring more news," Dummacos says sadly. "The king is also dead."

"The king?" asks another. "When?"

"We found his body today. Thieves ambushed him while he was on a secret mission. This day will forever be marked as a day of sorrow throughout Gaul in the hearts of all her people."

"So what do we do now, captain?" asks a third.

Dummacos draws his sword and says, "We serve King Litaviccos and Queen Sarah!" He kneels before them once more. The other soldiers draw their swords and kneel. Sarah simply walks to the first soldier, leans over and kisses him on his sweat laden forehead. "Thank you," she simply says. She then walks to the next soldier and does the same. She walks to each soldier while Dummacos and Litaviccos watch.

The men are breaking down the camp outside the cave. There are murmurs and whispers among them as they tie supplies to pack animals, load wagons and prepare to leave. Three of the soldiers carry Mary's wrapped body to a wagon to take it back to the palace. Sarah walks up to Dummacos while he is alone. "Tell me what happened here, captain," she quietly demands.

"What do you mean, my lady?" he responds nervously.

"Why did my mother die here? Why could no one come to see her?"

Dummacos hesitates for a moment and then slowly explains, "Vercingetorix wasn't a very caring man. But in your heart, you already knew that. The truth is, he was too greedy. He saw your mother as powerful and kept her here to usurp that power."

"So she *was* being held against her will," Sarah sighs. "I told Vio something was wrong."

"Litaviccos didn't know she was here," Dummacos adds. "Vercingetorix told virtually no one."

"You couldn't save her, captain?" Sarah asks suspiciously.

"I can tell you truthfully, she remained here because she would not leave without you. She was trapped here."

"Why trapped?" Sarah asks.

"You were Princess Sarah, my lady. She could not come to you and Vercingetorix would never let you leave. Not to mention leaving Litaviccos…"

"Oh yes, I see now," Sarah says with a slow heavy sigh. "We were both trapped in a way, I guess."

"All part of king's plan. When your mother got sick, I tried to get her some attention, but the king didn't allow it. He only did whatever would make himself stronger within the kingdom."

"Vio loved him," Sarah laments.

"Litaviccos was never allowed to see all the man he was. For his part, the king truly loved Litaviccos and would do anything to protect him. And Litaviccos did look up to him."

There was a pause as she looks into his eyes. "So you're saying that you tried to give her a way out?" Sarah asks. "Tell me the truth, captain."

"Truthfully," explains Dummacos, "I asked her, begged her, to leave and she wouldn't. She was always thinking about you."

Sarah then stares into his eyes for a time, looking for the truth she had been denied for so long, and asks, "You loved her, didn't you?"

Dummacos grows uncomfortable as he hesitates once more, but finally stammers, "Yes. Yes I did. For my part."

Sarah takes his large, rough hand between hers and says, "Thank you, captain. For everything you did for her." She leans in and kisses his cheek.

"It was my pleasure, my lady," Dummacos says bashfully.

A Time Of Justice

The new king and queen return to home. The news of the king's death spreads quickly. As the carriage nears the city led by Dummacos and his men, crowds gather on both sides of the road and stand cheering their new king and queen. Sarah looks into their eyes as they pass by and sees a new found glee that she had never seen before. It is in their faces and their cheers and their spirit that she finds the convicting evidence of who she had long suspected Vercingetorix was, and the kind of king that Dummacos had described. It is also a telling statement of the promise that Litaviccos holds to do what is right by the people. She could see in their eyes a new hope for their own future. But would Litaviccos ever be able to see that?

As they arrive at the palace, Sarah politely leaves Litaviccos to greet all his new subjects and as quietly as possible slips into the palace. There she is met by the nursemaid and she gathers her son into her arms once more. She holds him close to her breast and begins to cry. The nursemaid tries to console her, but she says that she will be fine and goes to find a quiet spot to rock her son and remember the woman that never got to hold him.

After several hours, Litaviccos finds Sarah in the nursery rocking little Calix. "I missed you," Litaviccos begins to say.

"Shhh," Sarah admonishes, "I just got him to sleep."

Litaviccos walks quietly over and sits down next to her. He reaches out and put his hand gently on the baby's head.

"Your subjects wanted to meet their new queen," he whispers.

"I know, but I'm not ready yet," she whispers back.

"I know. This all happen so fast. My father... your mother... and me king now? My head is still spinning."

"You will make a great king."

"You think so?"

"Better than even your father. He'll be proud of you."

"I don't know about that."

"Do you remember when I would say, 'I'm the princess, so my opinion is the only one that counts'?"

"Yeah..."

"Well, now I'm queen. So it counts double now."

Litaviccos begins to laugh. "Shhh..." Sarah says again. There is a silence that is only broken by the small sounds of a sleeping baby. Both of them smile.

"I'm sorry about your mother and there will be time to honor her, but I have to honor my father now," Litaviccos whispers.

"Of course," Sarah nods.

"Your mother will be honored..." Litaviccos continues.

"I know, Vio," Sarah interrupts. "It's alright. I do understand." Litaviccos leans over and kisses Sarah's cheek and then kisses his son lightly on his head.

It is a chilly overcast day, but the wind barely blows and there is a quiet stillness hanging over the city Litaviccos has never experienced before. He stands for a time on the balcony overlooking the plaza in front of the palace. Sarah stands beside him wrapped in a shawl against the chill. Litaviccos begins to say something several times, but the words get misplaced before they make their way out of his mouth. Sarah's thoughts are on Dummacos' comments at the cave and she can think of nothing at the moment to say to Litaviccos that would bring him solace. Instead, they both seem doomed to stand and stare. Below them, in the plaza, is a platform that holds the king's great stone coffin. People plod through the plaza to pay their respects; coming and going like leaves that are kicked up and blown about by the wind. Families moving in different directions; some stopping for a short time before moving on and some that pass straight through. Those that notice Litaviccos and Sarah would nod or wave.

"They look like they've been paid to come and give their final respects," Litaviccos says dejectedly. "Some seem truly sorrowful but many seem to be hanging around just to gossip and some fly by so fast, their small children are running."

Sarah wraps herself around his arm and lays her head on his shoulder, "Do not think harsh of them. He was not their father, he was only their king. Most of them may never have seen him while he lived."

"Yes," Litaviccos says placing his free hand up to her face, "you're right. I can't expect them to feel like me. I'm just feeling so lost now, Sarah. I don't think I can do this... not rule all of Gaul."

"God will bring us a solution. Jesus said, 'Do not let your heart be troubled'," Sarah reassures him.

"The council of clan kings... sorry, *governors* will meet in two weeks. They will be calling for my head. I know it. What will I do then?"

Sarah squeezes his arm, "I'm getting cold. I'm going inside." She turns to go back into the palace and Litaviccos follows her.

The next day, Dummacos enters the same balcony. "You sent for me, my lord?" Dummacos asks stiff and dutifully.

"Relax captain," Litaviccos says as he gazes out once more over the crowds passing by his father. He turns to address Dummacos, "You've been more help to me than you will ever know, captain. Now, I fear calling on you too many times as you may begin to think I'm incompetent." Litaviccos holds up his hand to silence Dummacos before he can object. "But, I am calling on you again. The council meets in less than two weeks. I'm at a loss for what I will tell them. You know their minds more than I do. What can I expect?"

"They will not be happy." Dummacos shakes his head.

"That much I do anticipate," replies Litaviccos. "What else?"

"You must not let them bully you. Whether they like it or not, they are still bound by their honor to uphold the agreement they signed with your father. You are – by all rights - ruler of all Gaul."

"But what if I don't want to be the ruler of all Gaul?"

"You must be, my lord," insists Dummacos.

"Why?" Litaviccos asks.

Dummacos hesitates. "Because you, of all the clan kings, have a chance to truly unite the people."

"My father united them, didn't he?" Dummacos bows his head and doesn't answer. "What is it?" Litaviccos implores. "Tell me."

"I'm sorry, my lord," Dummacos begins to explain. "But your father was not the man you thought he was. He hid most of his dealings from you. He was the most ruthless, scheming and greedy man to ever rise to lead a clan."

"What? How can you say that?" Litaviccos demands angrily.

"Why aren't you more prepared to be king? Why didn't he let you watch him? Why were you never allowed around him when he was conducting clan matters?" Dummacos asks. Litaviccos has no immediate answer. "He excluded you from all the things he should have been teaching you."

"He always said he was busy or that I was not ready," Litaviccos mumbles to himself.

"It was because he knew you would see him for what he actually was. For all his selfishness and greed, he did love you and would do anything for you. He wanted you to think of him as a great man."

"I remember Father complaining that no one ever understood his vision for Gaul." Litaviccos sits on a bench and stares lost into the sky.

"His vision was for him to control all of Gaul and step on anyone who got in his way," Dummacos says. Litaviccos continues to just stare. "The worst was when he kidnapped Mary."

Litaviccos snaps back to the moment, "Kidnapped? No, he was shielding her from the Romans."

"I'm sorry, my lord. But I was the one he gave responsibility to keep her there in that cave. I was to keep her alive until your father could figure out how to dispose of her quietly. Your father told me the whole plan."

"Dispose of her? Why?"

"He saw the opportunity to seize power from the other clans. Mary's influence - and now Queen Sarah's - is so powerful, he wanted it for himself."

"I don't understand," Litaviccos says shaking his head.

"With Mary out of the way, he could convince Sarah to marry you so he could claim her as his daughter. He then used that to force the other clan kings to give him all power or he would use those loyal to Mary to begin revolts inside their borders."

"I can't believe my father would do that," Litaviccos says in disbelief.

"Before he died, your father told me that he had learned that you were trying to go behind his back to find Mary."

"Yes, I did." Litaviccos admits sheepishly.

"What did you find out?"

"It was suspicious," Litaviccos says. "All of father's counselors either ignored me or told me not to get involved. But then one of the kitchen servants told me that the soldiers were sneaking her food." Dummacos nods. "I couldn't tell Sarah that... Sarah?" Litaviccos exclaims. "So we were tricked into marrying each other?"

"No. Your father knew you loved each other. He just used it to his advantage to get the other clan kings to submit to him. You and Sarah have been the only refreshing breath in this whole smelly business. That is why you must rule."

There is a long silence as Litaviccos sits and ponders. Finally he mutters, "How am I going to tell Sarah?"

"In my own opinion, my lord, I think it would be better if Sarah never learned of her mother's situation from you."

"Why? Shouldn't she know the truth?"

"To what end, my lord? If she believes *you* had any hand in this..."

"But I didn't!" Litaviccos interrupts.

"Yes, my lord. But if she even suspected that you did, you could lose her trust forever. She cannot love you any more than she does now. Leave the past in the past. At least, for now."

"Yes," Litaviccos sighs. "I think you're right. We will never speak of this again."

"Yes, my lord," Dummacos replies dutifully.

"And so," Litaviccos muses, "what about the meeting?"

"You father used your marriage to cheat the other clan kings. They are unaware that you now know the circumstances of the deal. They will say you are too young to rule and will ask that you break your father's deal. They will not let you cheat them too. You must be cautious. You are standing at the edge of war."

"I don't want to cheat them," Litaviccos agrees. "But I must do what's right for my own clan." Then Litaviccos sighs and puts his head in hands, "I just wish I knew what *that* was."

There is another long silence. And then Dummacos asks, "Will that be all, my lord?"

Litaviccos looks up at Dummacos and then stands up. "No, that will not be all," he says strongly.

"My lord?" Dummacos asks confused.

"You have served me so well. What do you say to becoming my personal advisor? You are a wise man. I could really use your counsel on a regular basis. You've been a soldier long enough. What do you say?"

"With respect," Dummacos hesitates, "it would be a great honor. But, I have been and always will be a soldier first. I admit that it would be nice not having to go sloshing around in the mud and muck. But it is where I am most comfortable... if you can understand."

"I understand," smiles Litaviccos. "So, I will make you a general instead. That way you can be both."

"General?" Dummacos says shocked. "Your father never wanted a general in his army. I think he thought it would take away from his own power. Or maybe he didn't trust anyone enough for that."

"Well, I trust you with my life and that of Sarah's. So, what say you ... *General* Dummacos?"

"Thank you, my lord. I will never make you regret this day."

"I believe you. Thank you, general. That will be all."

"Yes, my lord!" Dummacos says enthusiastically and exits back into the palace. Litaviccos turns to stare at the people again and sighs, "I just wish I knew what *that* was..."

A majority of the council has decided that this meeting will be at a place of their choosing, not Litaviccos'. The first king arrives early in the morning and the last one arrives just before dusk. Litaviccos and Sarah arrive just before lunch. The meeting is to convene the next morning and Litaviccos paces next to a desk in their room similar to one his father used to conduct all official business from. Sarah enters the room to check on him. She smiles, "Come to dinner, you're going to wear your feet down to nubs."

"I know what I want to do, but I don't know how I'm going to get the others to agree." Litaviccos says nervously.

"What do you want to do?" Sarah asks as she sits down in a chair.

"I want us to be a true council. Why can't we chart our destinies together?"

"Sit down, Vio. You're wearing *me* down," Sarah says. As Litaviccos sits, she asks, "Why can't you do that?"

"It's the same old problem we've always faced. Trying to get everybody to agree. We haven't had a very successful history of doing that," Litaviccos says sheepishly

"Ok. So, what are the real problems keeping everyone from getting along?"

"Well, from what I've gotten from my advisors, the biggest issue is the disputed territories my father has with just about every clan," Litaviccos explains. "My father, it seems, wasn't satisfied with having the biggest clan in Gaul. He was supposed to divide the disputed territories that my grandfather took by force during some temporary peace that the clans supposedly had, but that my grandfather didn't abide by... If that makes sense. My father kept putting it off. And the other kings are not ready to forget about it anytime soon."

"Well," Sarah says as she rises, "there will only be peace if everybody wants it bad enough. You have to make them believe that peace is worth more than war. But I'm sure you'll do what's right." Sarah's words sweep a new idea into Litaviccos's head. Suddenly he smiles. "Whatever you do, I'm sure it will be a kingdom our son will be proud of..." Sarah continues.

"That's it!" Litaviccos shouts as he jumps up from the chair.

"What's it?" Sarah asks perplexed. Litaviccos rushes to her and wraps her in his arms. He gives her a big kiss and then rushes back to sit at the desk. Sarah stands there stunned for a moment as Litaviccos begins writing. After the moment passes, Sarah mutters, "Does this mean you're not coming to dinner? Vio?"

The next morning, the clan kings stream into the meeting room amid greetings and jeering. They sit as their small entourage of servants begins to fill up the space around them. There is an uneasy air and many of the clan kings seem anxious. "Gentlemen," Litaviccos shouts and the chaos begins to cease, "let us get down to business."

Immediately Ambiorix jumps to his feet and proclaims angrily, "Your father is dead, Litaviccos. And I want you to break our agreement."

"We've decided, pup! All of us," Catuvolcos chimes in. "We're not taking orders from you. You're too young to command all of Gaul." Many of the kings add their voice and nod in agreement.

"I agree with you," Litaviccos says loudly but calmly.

"You agree?" Ambiorix asks confused. Several others also voice a disbelief in Litaviccos's agreement.

"You're quite right. I would be foolish to think I could rule all of Gaul with my limited experience. In truth, I don't want that much responsibility."

"So, you're breaking the agreement then?" Ambiorix asks.

"Not yet," replies Litaviccos. "I will break it when we have agreed to what will replace it."

"And what do want that to be?" Catuvolcos asks skeptically.

"I propose that we re-form the true council. Where all of us make decisions as equals."

There is a cacophony of comments between kings and one cries, "It never worked, that's how we ended up at war with each other."

Ambiorix laughs, "You expect us all to sit in a room together and talk?"

"Is that not what we're doing now?" Litaviccos replies. Another outbreak of comments. "I have recently become aware of how my father cheated you… how my grandfather cheated your grandfathers. I do not wish to cheat you, but I do not want war either."

"Why do I need to agree with Catuvolcos," jokes Ambiorix. "If I want his agreement, it's easier to just beat it out of him." This brings a hearty laugh from both kings and servants.

"Most of you," Litaviccos continues pointing to some of the kings, "you fight each other but you don't know why. You fight only because your fathers fought with each other because their fathers fought with each other. The Romans call us barbarians. It's time to prove them wrong. It's time to stop fighting among ourselves and carry the fight to those who truly oppress us. It's time to build clans that will give a chance to our children to grow old. I love my son, and I do not want him fighting my fights as you have fought your father's fights. Are you so heartless as fathers that you would pass onto them the violence that you continue without real reason or honor?"

"The pup makes sense," Catuvolcos grumbles. "Since we agreed to this deal and there has been a forced peace, I've spent more time teaching my seven-year-old son than I have spent with my other three older sons combined."

"But we've always fought. It's our way," explains Ambiorix.

"Maybe I'm getting too old then," laments Catuvolcos. "But the thought of returning to battle... the thought of seeing more of my clansmen, my brothers face down in the mud, never to teach our ways to our children... Just thinking about it turns my spit to vinegar in my mouth."

"I say it's worth a try," says Bituitus.

"And what if this is just another trick?" asks Ambiorix "What's in it for us except to keep us from attacking Litaviccos?"

"As a gesture of my faith in all of you," Litaviccos says, "I will surrender all of the disputed lands my father holds to the clans from which they were taken." There is a collective gasp among the kings. Litaviccos smiles and says calmly as he holds up a stack of parchments, "Unlike my father, I have already drawn up the documents to return your lands."

"Do you know what you're doing?" Catuvolcos asks. "That's about a fourth of your holdings."

"Consider it justice for what my forbearers have done," Litaviccos replies. "I wish to wash away the blood and begin with clean hands."

"It would appear he is committed to this, Catuvolcos," says Bituitus thoughtfully. "He's not all mouth, like his father. Perhaps this pup is wise beyond his years."

"And who will lead this council? You, Bituitus?" Ambiorix asks skeptically.

"Litaviccos will lead the council," Catuvolcos says.

"Litaviccos? Why?" asks Ambiorix.

"Do you trust me to lead it?" Catuvolcos inquires.

"No," Ambiorix says emphatically.

"Nor would I trust you," replies Catuvolcos. Then turning to Litaviccos says, "But I'll trust him. He has not been tainted by the greed of our rivalries like the rest of us. Furthermore, my oldest son will represent my clan on this new council. He has not seen that much war and he is not an old ox plowing his furrow like I am. Like Litaviccos, I'm finding that he has little taste for bloodshed."

"Yes," Bituitus agrees. "I will send my son to stand for our clan. Perhaps their youth will succeed where we have failed."

MARY REMEMBERED

Litaviccos manages to win over the majority of clan leaders easily. The rest are forced to take part or be left out. It will take time to build the trust needed, but the inexperience of the participants will make finding a new path less painful. The acquisition of the disputed lands is a big step to building the trust and hope returns to Gaul.

After returning home, Litaviccos commissions three of his best stonecutters to create a coffin for Mary. Like that of King Vercingetorix, the news of Mary's death spreads rapidly throughout the region. This time the sky is bright and the sun is high, but it is colder. People are bundled up tightly against a biting wind. Litaviccos again stands on the same balcony overlooking the plaza in front of the palace with Sarah wrapped in his arms. Mary's coffin rests on the same platform that his father's coffin occupied a few months earlier. It has a sculpted woman on the cover in a flowing robe and holding a bouquet of flowers. It is not as resplendent as the king's coffin, but Sarah is satisfied that Mary would have thought it was beautiful. This time, Litaviccos is not numb with grief, but stunned with amazement as the plaza is packed with people. Some of them stay for hours praying and weeping. There are people waiting all day to enter the plaza in a line that snakes its way through the city like a thick ribbon.

"There are so many people," Litaviccos says numbly.

"She must have touched a lot of hearts," sniffs Sarah.

"I wonder if you or I will be remembered like this," Litaviccos muses.

"It depends, I guess."

"Depends on what?"

"On how many lives we touch. On what kind of kingdom we leave to our children."

"Well, to a son at least," Litaviccos smirks.

"Maybe two," Mary whispers.

"Two? Are you with child again?" Litaviccos asks excitedly.

"Maybe."

"Maybe? What do you mean by maybe?"

"It's too soon to be sure, Vio. But with any luck..." Litaviccos gives her a hug and kisses her forehead. "I'm getting cold, let's go inside."

As they enter back into the palace, Sarah says, "I think I'm going to go lie down."

Litaviccos gives her one last hug and sends her on her way. He wanders into his state room where Viscount Gobannitio, is busy with work.

"It's amazing, Gobannitio," Litaviccos sighs.

Gobannitio ceases his work and asks, "What is amazing?"

"The amount of people who have come to see Mary," Litaviccos says as he sits at the table where Gobannitio is working. "There are ten times the number of people who have come to see her than came to see my father."

"The people loved her. She truly cared for them as well. It's hard to say how much power she had as queen or how many subjects she ruled in this Judea kingdom she came from."

"Queen?" Litaviccos scoffs. "She wasn't a queen. She was just a disciple of this man Jesus."

Now it is Gobannitio who is confused, "Your father never told you?"

"Told me what?"

"I'm sorry, my king. I thought he would have told you such an important secret."

"What secret? What are you babbling about?"

"Well, now that he is gone, I guess you should know. Your father told me that Mary shared her deepest secret with him. Mary was the wife of this king, Jesus."

"Wife? My father said that?"

"Yes. That is why she was so important to him. She was Jesus' wife and when Jesus was overthrown as king, she was exiled. That is how she ended up here. Sarah is the only bloodline of the true Jewish king."

"Why didn't Sarah tell me that?" Litaviccos asks bewildered.

"She may not know, my lord. You father said Mary kept the secret from everyone in order to protect herself and Sarah," Gobannitio explains. "She was afraid for both their lives."

"Is that why she has such a large following among the Jews?" Litaviccos muses.

"It is hard to tell, my lord. As I said, it is a closely guarded secret. If you wish to protect your queen, I would suggest you keep the secret. If those who exiled Mary find out that Sarah is here…"

"Yes, yes. I see what you're implying." Litaviccos says solemnly. He walks to the hallway and hastens one of his servants to him. He tells the servant, "Have General Dummacos meet me in the study."

Dummacos enters the study some time later and Litaviccos is pacing. "You sent for me, my lord?" Dummacos asks?

"Yes, general," Litaviccos says, "come in and sit down." After the both are seated, Litaviccos says, "I wish to discuss something with you. You have seen the crowds outside?"

"Yes. It is unexpected."

"Unexpected? It is amazing. To have so many people hold you in such high esteem... Some have been traveling for days. I can finally see what my father saw in her. She was more powerful and influential than most of us ever realized."

"I would be willing to say that Queen Sarah is as loved as Mary," Dummacos replies. "Maybe even more."

"That's what I'm worried about."

"I'm sorry, my lord, I don't follow..."

"I see it all so clearly now. I can see why Mary had to flee from jealous rulers in this place... *Judea*, where she came from. I can see how much power and influence a royal follower of this Jewish god can wield. I can understand why her own people would come after her."

"But she is gone now," Dummacos adds.

"Yes. But now I worry for Sarah and my son. I have to share this secret with you. You're the only one I can trust and I need your help. Gobannitio informed me of this secret my father kept. Mary was actually married to this man Jesus, who was a Jewish king."

"We spoke often while I was guarding her. She never mentioned that to me." Dummacos replies surprised. "But now that you mention it, I do remember your father speaking of a secret. When I asked, he would not tell me what it was."

"It was a secret she didn't even share with her own daughter."

"Sarah doesn't know? That would explain a lot. Why Mary was so concerned for her."

"No. I don't believe she knows. And I don't think I want her to know. I don't want this secret broken. I don't want Sarah to know that she might be hunted."

"You think her own people would come after her?"

"If she is the only bloodline of this Jesus... a king and the son of her god... How safe will she be here if people know the secret? How safe will she be anywhere? And my son, for that matter? He, too, is now a part of this bloodline."

"Are you saying we should send her away?" Dummacos asks concerned.

"No, no, no," Litaviccos shakes his head. "But we need to keep her secret as safe as possible. Everyone knows Mary and Sarah as disciples. That is the way I want to keep it. Only a handful of us now know that Sarah is a direct bloodline of this Jewish king. We must guard that secret at all costs. Not even Sarah must know the secret."

"Yes, my lord, I follow now. I will make it of high priority."

"We must keep it from the eyes of Rome, the other clans and all the Jews here in Gaul. Everyone must know them only as my wife and son. We must keep it from any Jews who might betray us to the powers of this Judea kingdom."

"Of course," Dummacos agrees.

"Thank you, general. As I've said before, I trust you with our lives."

Dummacos rises to leave and then pauses, "I will select a few of my most trusted men as a special guard to your family."

"Excellent idea, General Dummacos. But they must not be obvious. I do not want to draw extra attention to the matter. They will need to be a secret guard. I leave that to your discretion."

"Of course, my lord."

Litaviccos finds himself once again pacing the hallway when the door opens and he is allowed into the room.

"It's a girl, my lord," the midwife says as she gently plops the small bundle in Litaviccos's arms.

He pulls back the thin blanket to see a little, round, pink face. She begins to cry and fuss. Litaviccos walks over to the bed and sits down next to Sarah. "She's beautiful," Litaviccos whispers.

"I want to name her Mary," Sarah smiles.

"Yes," Litaviccos nods, "I think that Mary would be a wonderful name."

"She will be my reminder to these people so that they will never forget. I will teach her to be a disciple like my mother taught me." Sarah whispers to the new baby daughter in her father's arms, "Someday... Jesus will live on in you."

Litaviccos becomes lost in thought of the new revelation and what it will mean to all his children and their children for generations to come. "Yes," Litaviccos thinks, "Jesus will indeed live on in you."

"Vio?" Sarah says snapping him out of his thought. "If you'll give her to me, I'll feed her so she'll quit fussing."

Litaviccos says, "Oh... yes. Of course, dear." He kisses his daughter gently and passes her to Sarah saying, "I'll come check on you later." He walks from the room thinking to himself, "Poor Sarah. She will never know that she is the bloodline to this Jewish king. This secret will be ours to protect forever; as long as a new generation is spawned of this bloodline. I guess that there will always be those in each generation that will have to be trusted with the secret and with the protection of those who shall live unknowingly in its shadow. Maybe a day will come when my family will be able to tell the world this secret and my children may one day be restored to the Jewish thrown. Now, I have to protect her, our children and all of our generations to the best of my ability so that the secret of Mary Magdalene will never pass from us."

About The Author

Dave Dillon has spent his whole life on this earth, at the time of this writing, as a Texan. He is mostly a computer geek and a Pastor in the United Methodist Church. He enjoys science fiction, Christian fiction, history and theology. Especially where any or all of these overlap.

91043882R00120

Made in the USA
Columbia, SC
13 March 2018